All We Have

The Survivor Journals, Book Three

Sean Patrick Little

Spilled Inc. Press
Sun Prairie, Wisconsin
© 2018

Copyright 2018 Sean Patrick Little

Published by Spilled Inc. Press
Sun Prairie, Wisconsin
Email: spilledincpress@gmail.com
On Twitter: @SpilledIncPress

All rights reserved.
ISBN-13: 978-1-387-90747-2

Cover Design: Paige Krogwold © 2018

Printed in the U.S.A.

All We Have

The Survivor Journals, Book Three

By Twist

To Hope

It's Thursday, I think. Honestly, it doesn't matter.

It's amazing how little I think about the calendar now. Once, it ruled my life: Was it Sunday night? Did I have my homework done? Did I have a three-day weekend this week? How many more days until Christmas? How many more days until Summer Break?

Now, it's just an archaic thing, a remnant of the old days, an arbitrary way of marking the passage of time. I haven't known what day of the week it was for more than a year and a half, not since the Flu killed nearly everyone on the planet.

I survived the first year in Wisconsin, weathering a rough winter by scavenging supplies from stores and homes, burning wood for heat. I left Wisconsin for the South, traveling to New York, Washington D.C., and down the eastern seaboard looking for other survivors. I found Renata Lameda in New York. She came south with me, and we have settled outside of Houston, Texas.

Now it's not about surviving; it's about building a future, come what may.

This is the continued journal of my life.

My name is Twist. I'm almost twenty. I've never been a wilderness guy, nor have I gardened, farmed, or raised animals. All that is going to have to change if I want to live in this world devoid of civilization.

The only important thing is that Renata and I are still alive.

Part One
Spring

CHAPTER ONE

The Mighty Nimrod

I have always believed that most people either did something, or they didn't do something. It doesn't matter what that thing is, pick a thing at random: Skiing, for example. You either ski, or you don't ski. And if you do ski, then you likely didn't just wake up one day and think, "Hey! I should ski." Usually, if you do something, it's because you were somehow indoctrinated into it, sometimes it's by your friends, or a TV show, but it's usually done by your family. If your mom and dad ski, then you likely had sticks on your feet shortly after you learned to walk. If your mom and dad were bowlers, then you probably played video games in the game room of the lanes on Friday nights when they bowled league, and you probably started bowling in kids' leagues, too. You either do a thing, or you don't, and if you don't do something, it can be really hard to start doing it.

I bring this up because I am *not* a hunter. Not in the least. My parents were not outdoorsy. My mom's idea of "roughing it" was a hotel without room service. The closest my dad got to nature was mowing the lawn once a week in the summers. We didn't fish. We didn't hunt. I don't even remember going to the zoo. (*I know we went, because there were photos of it, but it precedes my memory by a few years. I was still in diapers when we went.*) Two years ago, my only knowledge of hunting came from flipping channels on cable TV on Saturday mornings and pausing briefly on the Outdoor Network as two bearded dudes in blaze orange took down a buck with rifles. And Wisconsin is a hunting paradise! People treat the opening day of Deer Season like a religious holiday. I remember opening days where half my classmates were missing because they were out at deer camp. The only reason I was able to remain so deficient in hunting knowledge and skills was because my parents did not do it.

All that changed two years ago, though. The Flu happened. Humanity died. All across the globe, primates withered and died, drowning in fluids accumulating in their lungs. For whatever reason, I did not die. A rare immunity? Dumb luck? A curse? I do not know. All I know is that I waited to die, and I'm still here. I have a need to eat, and two years into the apocalypse, the wealth of prepackaged and canned food stores are starting to grow thin, what was produced before the Fall of Man is starting to spoil, and thus, to survive, I must learn to hunt.

It is little things like this where I wish I knew someone who could help me learn to hunt, indoctrinate me into it, teach me how to do it properly. I have read books and magazines on hunting. Mostly magazines. I acquired a stack of *Outdoor Life* and *Field & Stream* from a library, and I spent two solid weeks devouring every article in them. Between that and what scraps I've gleaned over the years from books like the "Little House" series and *Where the Red Fern Grows*, I hope I have learned enough to be a decent provider.

I'm not alone in the apocalypse; not anymore, at least. About nine months back, I found a petite spitfire of a Brooklyn girl in New York City, and she joined me on my journey south. Renata, or "Ren" as she prefers, has become my reason for living. Over the trip from New York to

Houston, Texas, I guess you could say we fell in love. It's the same old story, really:

-*Boy Meets Girl*

-*Boy Falls for Girl*

-*Girl Thinks Boy is Gay*

-*Boy Gets Mauled By Tiger*

-*Girl Saves Boy's Life*

-*Boy and Girl Realize They Love Each Other and Settle Down on a Burgeoning Farm in a Post-Apocalyptic Entropy-Ridden Wasteland.*

You know—that old chestnut.

Late last fall, Ren and I made it to a little farm along the shore of Lake Houston, about twenty miles northeast of the city of Houston. We did it just in time, too. Gas reserves were starting to deplete and go sour. After a period of time, what gas was left in ground tanks evaporated enough that it began to turn gelatinous. Gelatinous gas was no good for powering internal combustion engines. It would still burn all right; it just wouldn't get pumped through pistons to power a machine. My trusty, beloved Jayco Greyhawk RV now sits on the edge of our property on flattened tires, never to run again. It still works well as a writing refuge, though. I spend some time in there every day working on my journal, hacking and clacking at the typewriter until all these thoughts I have in my brain work their way out. I find it cleansing. Plus, should society ever rebuild itself, or should aliens ever find the wreckage of our once-proud civilization, maybe they will be able to learn something useful about how we few survivors lived after the Flu.

Maybe I'm just wasting my time. Who knows?

Ren and I spent our first winter in Texas fixing up the farm. Being a Wisconsin boy, the Texas winter was appreciated greatly. It rarely got below fifty. There was only one flurry all winter, and it melted within eight hours. I never wore anything heavier than a light jacket. At no point did I fear freezing to death. It was a welcome change to battling the cold of the Midwest. A friend of my dad's moved to Phoenix years ago. When my dad asked why he was leaving Wisconsin, he said, "Because you don't have to shovel sunshine." I understand his thinking now. Winter has its good points, but in the thick of winter, it is hard to remember them.

The house we found and chose as our home did not need a lot of work. It was a newer home, still in good condition. Luckily, no one died in the home, so it was free of that lingering smell of death that houses with corpses in them acquired. That was an imperative for our new home. Also imperative: enough space to grow a large garden and tend to crops, space and housing for animals we might return to domestication, and close enough proximity to the lake for me to figure out a way to get us fresh water. We found all of this in a little, modern house with a large barn behind it, some pasture land, and a view of the lake.

We cleared debris from the yard. I used a large hand-scythe to hack down the overgrown weeds and make a livable space. I found an old-fashion, push mower, the kind without an engine, and I used that to winnow down the yard to a livable length. We aired out the house, opening windows and letting the prairie winds blow through to make the house feel alive and vibrant again. We settled into the master bedroom together, and started amassing the things we would need to make a life for the next sixty years: Clothes, linens, and a stockpile of guns and ammunition. (Luckily, given that we were in Texas, these things were all plentiful.) We raided a library for books, both fiction and non-fiction. We would need things to read. We would need reference materials to help us do things we did not understand. I found a book about using solar panels to take your home "off the grid." Given that "the grid" no longer existed, I figured it would be a useful book to have. That book gave us the possibility of having electric power again. That mean lights. That meant refrigeration. That meant a hot water heater. That meant we could power the well pump and have running water in the house again. That meant we could be civilized again. No more bathing in the yard with a washcloth and a cauldron of fire-heated water.

The RV got us back and forth to Houston several times during those first two or three months, more than enough for us to scavenge stores for everything we thought we would possibly need for the next sixty years.

We stored tools in the garage of the home, stacking them in piles. We also scavenged all the cordwood we could, making long, elegant rows along the edge of the yard, fuel for fires, fuel for cooking. I built a nice, stone-and-daub wood-fired oven from a kit, placing it near the back door. We had a fire pit in the yard, too. Between the two fires, our cooking needs were met.

Until I figured out how to hook up enough solar panels to give us some sort of electrical flow, we would have no heat in the house. We struggled through the winter by huddling together under heavy blankets on the coldest nights, but for two people from the northern states, we did not find the Texas winter all that intimidating. I came from a home where windows were opened at night as long as it was above fifty degrees. "Good sleeping weather," my dad would have said. At its worst, the Texas winter was a little uncomfortable and sort of annoying. At its best, it was like comfortable spring weather in Wisconsin.

It was hard to predict what we would need from week to week, let alone what we would need from year to year or decade to decade. We only knew that we would need a lot of things because resupply would eventually be difficult, if not impossible.

We were not going to go hungry anytime soon, so that was one thing we did not have to worry about. Canned food was still plentiful. We were slowly scavenging as much as we could from the homes around the lake, and if necessary, there were always more homes. However, canned and boxed food, or the prepackaged, carb-heavy snacks and easy eats that had a seemingly limitless shelf life were getting boring and repetitive. The salt used to preserve. Fresh vegetables and fruits, those that we could harvest from the land around us, were very welcome. We found a few fruit trees and a grove of avocado trees nearby. Ren planted tomatoes when we first moved in, and we found garlic and onions growing in the woods. Ren has kept me hip-deep in fresh guacamole for weeks. I could live on guacamole.

We have also started building up sustainable methods of keeping ourselves in fresh food. We managed to coral a couple of chickens that had been living in the wild. While skittish at first, they now seemed grateful to given a safe place to sleep at night and a fenced-in run for daytime grazing. Those chickens have been providing us with eggs. When we get a cockerel, we will be able to increase the flock and someday soon, we might be frying our own chickens.

Ren had grand plans to capture and breed rabbits for meat, but so far, that had not happened. Wild rabbits were hard to catch and keep alive, but we could see strains of rabbits that were once domesticated who now roamed wild. She built a small hutch and a fenced-in yard with a grate across the bottom to keep the little devils from tunneling out. She had live snares in the woods nearby, but so far, she had only managed to capture squirrels, a couple of opossums, and a very perturbed raccoon—nothing that we really considered immediately necessary as cuisine, really.

I had managed to grab a pair of Holstein cows that were wandering the plains around the lake. Cows were never wild creatures. They were bred down from wild Aurochs and, over centuries, turned into the gentle-eyed, supremely chill beasts we know today. The two I caught weren't starving, but they did look ill. They were thin, despite the ample grasslands for forage. I was able to wrangle them with minimal roping skill. Okay, *no* roping skill. One just let me walk up and put a rope around her neck without a fight.

Once I lassoed the first one, the other just followed it back to the barn. A broad course of deworming paste I plundered from a vet's office got the cows back to their old selves, and they quickly began putting on weight and acting far more spry. Well, as spry as cows get, I guess. It's hard to tell with them. I like cows. They are mellow as hell. I've decided that people should be more like cows. Got a problem? Just stand there and chew your cud. It ain't the end of the world.

Of course, once I had cows, I leaned the joy of "mucking out stables." Frankly, after a week of that, I briefly considered turning them loose again. Ren wouldn't hear of it, though. Their manure became part of our necessary compost for plowing into land and keeping our farmland well fertilized. We named the cows Thing 1 and Thing 2. It was disappointing that they appeared to be still young, so they were not bred and producing milk, but if I could ever manage to find a bull, we might try to remedy that situation. We had initially considered eating them, but they were so sweet and gentle, they became more like pets. Ren and I resignedly decided they would not be meat unless we absolutely *had* no other choice but to eat them. Meat could come from elsewhere.

Which brings me back to hunting.

I spent most of the morning lying prone on top of a grassy hill, mostly hidden by knee-deep blades of grass. I had a long rifle with a scope tucked solidly into my shoulder. I have no idea if the scope is sighted properly, nor do I have any idea of how to do it. I should get a book about it, or find magazine articles about it. All I know of guns, really, is that you point one end at your target, squeeze the trigger, and then hope the gun doesn't snap back and smash you in the nose.

I was doing my best to hunt, though. I was hoping for a deer, or maybe a wild pig, or maybe even a cow, if necessary. Growing up in Wisconsin, I was around hunters a lot. I listened to talk of hunting. I heard hunting stories. I used to have to listen to my classmates debate different types of guns and ammunition. I should have paid more attention.

Most hunting stories started with "So there I was…" and ended with a poorly mimicked sound of gunfire, a vivid description of where the bullet hit the target, and then how long it took the hunter to track the target down if it ran after being hit. Then, weights of the beast and/or number of points of the antlers were tossed out to the listeners for comparison to their own legendary kills. Since I was not a hunter, nor did I ever believe I was going to be a hunter, I usually tuned out shortly after "So there I was…"

So there I was, atop the hill with a gun, and waiting for some poor, soon-to-be-dinner creature to happen into my field of view. I was choosing the "sit and wait" approach to hunting, rather than stalking my prey because, frankly, I'm lazy. The Texas sun was warm on my back and my legs, the dusty, dry smell of the prairie was welcoming, and the wind felt good on my face. Plus, hunting was a legitimate excuse to take a morning off of busting my tail on the farm. I did not mind the farm work, but it was definitely strenuous, and I'm a born-and-raised suburban soft-boy type whose hands had never known a callous until we settled on the ranch.

I was not a hunter. In two years of surviving the fall of man, I had only killed one creature, and that had been a cow that had been mauled by a group of wild dogs. It was suffering and dying slowly. I ended its misery from point-blank range. I don't think that really counts in terms being a mighty Nimrod.

In the fields below the little hill, I was watching a worn game trail. At one point, it might have been a place where cattle herds walked to pasture, but over the last two years, it had started to be reclaimed by the land. It was still visible, but a fine green fuzz of grass and weeds was finally starting to poke up through the hard-packed clay of the path.

After what felt like hours, but had probably only been forty or fifty minutes, I started to see movement in the tall grass around the trail. Something was coming. It was obviously not large game, but it might be edible. A turkey would be welcome, so would grouse or pheasant. I felt my pulse begin to elevate. I rocked into a better position, bringing up my right leg slightly to provide the feeling of a more stable base. I raised the rifle, elevating the barrel with my left hand and keeping the stock tight into my shoulder with the right. My mouth went dry. My heart began to race. I began to understand why people seemed to enjoy hunting. There was an anticipation to it, an excitement. *What was coming? What will happen next?*

The grass began to part, a dozen brown-and-white striped blobs emptied onto the game trail in a hodge-podge of grunts and awkward stumbles. Peccaries. In Texas, they were commonly called javelinas, and they looked like dwarf versions of wild boars, but hairier. In the right light, they were almost cute. I knew from reading issues of *Field & Stream* in the library back in Wisconsin that they were edible. In Portugal, rural families often raised them for food. I didn't have a recipe for cooking peccary handy, but I figured they were close enough to pigs that it would be similar. I wagered they'd be downright tasty with barbeque sauce, although to be fair—not much in this world *isn't* improved with barbeque sauce. I could put that stuff on cereal.

I tensed up. I did not want to miss. One loud crack of the rifle would be all I would be able to get. Once that thing roared, every animal within a two miles would promptly do an about-face from my position and start running. I sighted down the scope and found the fat male in the lead of the squadron. *(I'm not being hyperbolic: the collective noun for javelinas is "squadron.")* The male was lazing, not in any sort of a hurry. The rest of them followed his lead. They rooted. They sniffed. A couple of them rolled in the short grass, writhing to scratch their backs.

I reminded myself that I was not committing any sort of crime. I was an omnivore. They were food. Ren and I had no fresh meat at home. This was the way of the world, I told myself. Apex predators preyed upon prey. Taking a single javelina out of the world was not going to deplete the species. Even prior to the Flu, javelinas were something of a nuisance in Texas.

I lined up the male's head in the crosshairs of the scope. I took a deep breath and blew it out slowly, calming my heart rate. I took another breath and held it. The male paused, almost as if he sensed impending doom. It was now or never. I squeezed the trigger and the gun bucked and roared. My ears were ringing. At the base of the hill, the squadron scattered, the fuzzy blobs darting every which way for cover, legs churning like windmills.

Except for one.

A single blob lay still on the trail, a red stain on the side of its head.

Direct hit.

My heart stopped. I didn't know if I should scream, run away, or wet myself. I was stunned. I was in shock. I did it. *I actually did it!* I hunted!

It was only then that I realized my shoulder was killing me. The recoil of the rifle had been far more than I had anticipated. I really should practice with these things. The muscles in my arm hurt. My ears hurt. The world was muffled and faint-sounding. I should have used earplugs.

I slung the rifle onto my left shoulder—the one that didn't hurt—and walked down the hill toward my kill. I was prepared for field-dressing the thing, at least. I used a sharp hunting knife I'd been carrying since Wisconsin to open the cavity, remove the testicles, and cut out the organs. I left the gut pile in the field. Coyotes and buzzards will love me for it, I'm sure. The little peccary weighed somewhere between sixty and seventy pounds before the field dressing. After, he was still a weighty little thing, a compact forty or fifty pounds. I used a length of cord I carried in my pocket to loop him up by his legs so I could carry him a little easier. I threw him over a shoulder and set off for home. I could feel him bleeding onto my back and my jeans. Ren would probably throw a fit about that, and I couldn't blame her. We both did the laundry, and washing clothes by hand was no picnic. Maybe the sight of fresh meat would make her forget it. It was a brave new world, and we were bound to get a little dirty in it.

My mountain bike came with me from Wisconsin. I love that bike. While it was tethered to the back of the RV, I did not use it much, but once gasoline went to bunk, I was so glad to have that bike. The roads in Texas were still in surprisingly good condition. The lack of weather fluctuation in the North absolutely destroyed the highways and byways. Frost heaves and heat buckles were everywhere. With no road crews to fix potholes or repair major damage, the entropy that would eventually claim all the roads was only hastened. In Texas, the biggest thing I could see happening was the grass and occasional weed sprouting from the cracks in the asphalt. It was the start of the breakdown of the roads, I knew, but it would take longer down here.

One of the first things I did when we set up shop on the farm was to get a big cart that hooked onto the back of my bike. When I couldn't find one big enough in the bike stores around Houston, I used the frame of one to build a bigger one by putting down a plywood bed and making a cage of two-by-fours around it. On one side, there were hinges so it could open like a door for easier loading and unloading. Once the RV died, the bike became a vital piece of machinery for me on the farm, every bit as important as a rake, a hoe, and a hammer.

There were plenty of houses around the farm to scavenge for supplies. Once the homes were ransacked of usable goods, there were couches to tear apart for firewood or walls to tear down for studs. The houses would continue to give us usable goods for years, and I was grateful for that. However, there were tens of thousands of homes within bike-riding distance of the farm, and then the city of Houston beyond that. Houston, by road, was probably thirty or thirty-five miles from the farm. It was close enough that I could be there by bike in two or three hours. I could get up early, cycle to the city, loot a few stores, and be back at the farm by dinner, an exhausting day in the Texas heat, but not too difficult that it wasn't out of the question.

No matter how useful the bike was, and no matter how many tires, inner tubes, and cans of lithium grease I stockpiled in the garage for repairs, the bike was subject to entropy and would eventually break down. I had already grabbed a couple of new bikes and had them on a rack on the wall of the garage for when the inevitable happened. It might take a decade or two for the bike to go down, but it would eventually. I guess that's why I started looking at horses.

In the world before the Flu, horses were an expensive, impractical hobby for most of the people I knew in Wisconsin who owned them. I was always impressed by horses when I got to see them up close, but I never gave them a second thought. They were not part of my world. Now I had a farm with cows and chickens. A horse would be a very good addition to my world. A horse could be ridden, could pull a cart, or pull a plow. That would be very practical and necessary. I had no idea how to get a horse, though.

I saw herds of horses ranging around the grassy fields between Houston and the farm. The horses, probably freed from domestication during the Flu, had done very well for themselves. They had quickly banded together in groups for protection and procreation. I saw many foals trailing behind placid mothers. Alpha-male stallions led the herds, and anytime they were close to the road where I was riding, the stallions would swagger toward me, eying me suspiciously until they felt I was far enough along the road to no longer be a threat to their ladies.

I tried approaching a herd once. A pair of foals, curious and wide-eyed, were near the asphalt, and when I stopped to watch them play, they started moving closer to me. I got off my bike and moved slowly toward them. I stopped a safe distance from them and held out my hands. I spoke in a low voice and tried to coax them to coming toward me. Those foals had never seen a human in their lives. They walked closer, tentative and curious, but cautious. When the stallion saw his progeny moving toward the unwelcome biped, he charged me. I saw a flash of dappled gray out of the corner of my eye, and a mountain of horseflesh was steaming toward me, head low and teeth bared. I started to back up in a hurry. The stallion was faster than I was. He was on me in a second, so I dove to the side, hit the ground, and rolled. The stallion flashed past me and wheeled about for a second pass. I ran in the opposite direction of the herd until the stallion was satisfied with my retreat. Then, and only then, did he merge back with the herd, but he kept an eye on me until I rode away on my bike. When I was a hundred yards down the road, I heard the big stallion whinny a challenge at me. If I spoke horse, I would bet it he was saying something in a tough-guy voice, something like, *Yeah, keep walking, chump!* He bested me, and he knew it. That moment put the pipe dream of capturing one of those animals out of my head for a couple of weeks.

In my travels around the Texas plains, I saw a lot of horses and a lot of cows. They were everywhere, it seemed. After a few weeks of scavenging, I started to recognize different groups, each denoted by the stallion that led them. I also saw a lot of things you would not think you would see on the Texas plains: a quartet of elephants, a flock of ostrich, a couple mobs of emus, the occasional mating pair of giraffes, a caravan of dromedary camels—at least thirty of them—and a mob of kangaroos. In the waning days of the Flu, as people realized they were doomed, many zookeepers or wild animal park workers knew that the animals for which they cared were doomed if they were not freed from their enclosures. It might not have been ecologically sound in every case, but the rules of ecology went out the window when the dominant species that *wrote* the rules checked out of the planet. Most of the animals did very well. They kept to themselves. They foraged. They procreated. They prospered. Even cattle, which were *never* wild animals, figured out a way to keep living. Michael Crichton was right: Life *does* find a way.

Every so often, usually at night, Ren and I would hear a lion's roar. That was unsettling. Lion roars were very loud, and on a still night the sound could carry five or six miles, easily. It was a reminder that any still-living humans were no longer the apex predators. Even with a gun handy, a surprise lion attack would be difficult to survive. I even outfitted the cage on the bike cart to carry a shotgun in a sleeve so it would be in close enough proximity to me that I would have time to retrieve it if I saw one of the big cats. I was not worried about them coming into the farm, though. The fire we usually had burning in the fire pit was an excellent deterrent, and there was more than enough easy prey in the larger world for them. Still, I made plans to build a stockade wall around the farm at some point. That would be a monumental chore, but I would sleep better at night if I knew that Leo the Light-pawed Lion was not skulking around the barn upsetting Thing 1 and Thing 2. I would add it to the ever-expanding list of things that needed to be done.

I made future plans for domesticating some of the animals I saw roaming around the farm. Ostriches and emus could be used for meat and eggs. I've even heard that their skin makes good leather. I don't know what I'd do with emu leather, but I'm sure it might be useful someday. Kangaroos are probably good eating; I'm sure the Aboriginals probably ate 'roo. It might not be the tastiest thing on the planet, but beggars can't be choosers, and since the local Kroger's was no longer functioning, I would take my protein where I could get it.

I used my bike to haul scads of fencing material back to the farm. I pounded posts, put up crossbars and chicken wire, and made several large paddocks, just in case I would have the good fortune to capture a new animal that might benefit us in the long run.

I bring all this up because, as I hiked back to the farm with the peccary bleeding down my back, I saw a horse that I thought I might have a chance of capturing. It was a beautiful mare, small for an adult. I know horses get measured for height in a unit called "hands"—like, that horse is sixteen hands tall—but, but I have no idea how to measure a horse in "hands." This horse was smaller than most horses I've seen, but it was still clearly an adult horse. She was a bay horse, dark brownish-red body and black mane and tail. I have no notion of breeding and what makes a Quarter Horse different from an Arabian horse or anything else, so I could not tell you what breed she was. I know some colors. I know some breed names. I know that draught horses are the big monster horses, and that Thoroughbreds are fast. Other than that, I am a horse newbie. I know they're pretty, and they can be useful when domesticated and broken to ride and drive carts. The bay I saw seemed to be running solo. She was standing in the middle of a field placidly eating grass when I first saw her. I crested a small rise in the field and there she was, barely twenty yards from me. There was no herd around her, which I found strange. Horses are herd animals by nature. Solitary horses in the wild were fodder for predators. There was safety in numbers. I could not even see a herd anywhere in the vicinity. It seemed odd.

I froze in my spot and watched her. She watched me, too. There was no fear or concern in her eyes. She seemed to accept my presence. Slowly, I slipped the peccary off my shoulder and laid it in the grass. I laid the rifle next to the carcass. Cautiously, I took a couple of slow, easy steps toward the mare, my hands raised. She continued to watch me, head raised, ears twitching. After I closed the gap between us by half, she started to move. I froze again. She took two steps backward, then moved forward a step. The lack of fear told me she had once been owned, once been loved. She had been someone's horse. I took two more steps, then froze. She watched me carefully. I took another step. I was nearing touching distance. I watched her face for signs of annoyance or anger. Her large, black eyes just continued to watch me curiously. I held my hand out toward her. Cautiously, she leaned her long neck forward and snuffled at my hand. I could feel her hot, wet breath on my skin. It sent shivers up my spine. After a moment, she pulled back and cropped another mouthful of grass from the sea of green around us. I moved another step closer. I leaned my hand out and touched her neck, feeling heat and solid muscle beneath her fine coat.

I had no rope or halter to put on her, and no way of getting her back to the farm at the moment, unless she chose to follow me, which she did not. When I stepped back toward the javelina and my rifle, she decided that was the moment to turn and mosey off to other pastures. I watched her walk away from me and felt sad that I wasn't prepared to bring her home that day, but I knew she was around now. I could spend time looking for her, and maybe even catch her. If I could break her to ride or pull a cart or even plow, a horse would be worth her weight in canned food. I made the vow to bring that horse to the farm.

CHAPTER TWO

Ren

It's Thursday, I think…

I have no idea why Twist starts all his journals like that. I think it's stupid. Who cares what day it is? It's just another day, and the Gregorian calendar stopped existing the day no one in Greenwich was alive to take care of time. That's the reality of the world: a day is a day a day. Today will blend into tomorrow, and tomorrow will blend into the day after tomorrow. Sunrise, sunset. Seasons pass. It all becomes a blur, and tracking them no longer serves a purpose.

My name is Renata Lameda. Don't call me Renata. Ren is fine. I won't punch you if you call me Renata, but it's such a weird name. Years ago, my mother confided in me that Renata was a family name from my father's side of the family (he was Venezuelan), and she never really liked it. She wanted to name me "Trixie" after the Trixie Belden books she loved as a child. I don't know if that would have been any better. Unless I'd become a stripper. Trixie was a good stripper name. Or a magician. Trixie would be a good name for a female magician, too.

I'm twenty-three now. I was almost twenty-two when the flu hit. I'm soon going to be twenty-four. I feel old. As far as I know, I can legitimately claim to be the world's oldest woman. That just helps make me feel older.

I don't know why Twist writes these journals. He says it helps him clear his head, and he says it will be good to have a history of the world after the Flu. I think he's probably full of it, but it does give me something to do at night, and maybe that's worth it. Twist says I don't have to write every detail like he does, but for some reason it feels like it's competitive, like I need to write as much as he does, if not more.

This is the first entry in my journal. Until I met Twist, keeping a journal had never even occurred to me. Who would be around to read it? What was the point? If nothing else, Twist said that writing was therapeutic. We both have endured a lot. I guess having an outlet for all that trauma and frustration is a good thing.

Most of the past two years has been a blur. My parents died in the Flu. My brother was sickly, had cerebral palsy, and died shortly after my parents died because of his diseases and lack of medical care. He, like me and my sister, was immune to the Flu. My sister died at the hands of a group of psychos in New York when she and I were out scavenging for food. I was hiding in the shadows when they did. I had to watch her die. That was a dark time for me, but I came out of it, I guess. And I'm still here. *That what doesn't kill you, makes you stronger*, right?

I'm glad I'm in Texas with Twist, though. If it hadn't been for him, I'd probably still be in Brooklyn trying to carve out some sort of existence. Maybe I'd be dead. Maybe the friggin' Patriots would have captured me and turned me into some sort of slave for them. Maybe I would have gotten sick of the city and set out on foot or by bike to New Jersey or Virginia or something. Who knows? My dad always said that you have to play the hand you're dealt, and this is how I'm playing that hand.

I met Twist in Brooklyn almost a year ago. He seemed like a decent guy. Real simple. Real sweet. Easy-going. He was non-threatening. He looked scared, like me. There was something about the fear I could see in him that made me think he understood me and what I was feeling. It made me think that he'd keep me safe. And maybe I thought I could keep him safe, too. It drew me to him. I can't explain it.

Since then, we've grown close. Very close. I love him. I do. I'm confident that he loves me, too. But, what is love? It's a chemical reaction two people experience influenced by proximity and hormones. He's barely twenty. His hormones are crazy. I'm a healthy young woman. My hormones aren't to be trusted, either. Just a pair of crazy kids with no rules and no supervision, I guess. Things happen. I wonder about love, though. Sometimes, you hear people say, *I wouldn't love you if you were the last person on Earth.* For all intents and purposes, he and I are almost literally the last people on Earth. There are at least a few other people out there, but we don't know them, and they don't know us, and we're trapped in our own little world like Adam and Eve, or the Swiss Family Robinson.

When I was younger, I used to believe in soulmates. Every person had one perfect person out there for them. I blame Disney for that. One too many princess movies, right? Obviously, as I got older, I stopped believing in that stupidity. I used to laugh at girls in my neighborhood who called their boyfriends their "soulmates." Eight billion people roaming the Earth and the *one perfect person* for you ends up living in your neighborhood and going to your high school? What are the odds? I learned that relationships were work, and there was no such thing as a perfect mate. You should for someone who meets a lot of your ideal checklist points, and then round up to perfect. If it hadn't been for the Flu, Twist and I never would have met. I'm confident in saying that. He would have stayed in the Midwest. I would have stayed in New York. Our paths never would have crossed, and if they did, it would not have been in a meaningful way where we would have ended up falling in love.

So, of course, being a naturally insecure mess, despite the fact that insecurity is stupid *(especially in this post-Flu world)*, I wonder about this whole situation that he and I have going on. Would he love me if there was another woman around here? Would I love him if there was another man around here? If it hadn't been for the Flu, would he and I ever have matched with each other in the normal world where we would want to cohabitate or marry? I lay awake at night torturing myself with these thoughts. It's stupid, I know, but this is a journal and you're getting the best and worst of me. I'm not gonna sugar-coat it for you.

Twist seems endlessly decent and good. I hate that about him, sometimes. He wants to do right, always. He wants to be a good man. He wants to provide. He wants to make me happy. It makes me feel like I can never be his equal in that department. Is that just how people from Wisconsin are, or is he special that way? When I think about it, in my darkest thoughts, I think that he would love me if there were other women around, but because his goodness intimidates me at times, I don't know if I would love him if there were other options, and that makes me feel like crap, like he deserves better than me.

It also bothers me that I've taken peeks at his journals, and he doesn't obsess on this stuff like I do.

Stupid, Ren. Don't be stupid.

Anyhow, I'm trying to be positive about this whole situation. That's what Twist does. He looks around and says, "Hey, it could be worse." And then he tries to make whatever is wrong better. I've been trying to do that, too. I don't know if I can do it as well as he can, though.

At least we have a nice house.

When I was little, I used to dream about having the sort of house I live in now. I grew up in Brooklyn. When I was little, we lived in an apartment. When I got older, we moved to a row house. It wasn't too bad, but when you would see pictures of those luxurious McMansions in *Better Homes & Gardens* or *HGTV Magazine*, it just never felt like it was any good. We used to mock those suburban castles. We used to make up stories about how all the people who lived in them were lottery winners or something. We were just jealous. There's something to be said for living in the city, don't get me wrong, but you always want what you don't have, I guess. I wanted a house with a sprawling yard, and maybe a place for animals. I have that now. I have all the space and land I've ever wanted. It makes me deliriously happy. I wake up in the morning and look out over an actual yard. Maybe it's not a fancy, manicured lawn, but it's not overgrown, either. And it's mine. Ours, I should say. Me and Twist. I'm not used to speaking of us as a couple in the plural. Usually, you only do that to your girlfriends, and I don't have any of those anymore.

The loneliness gets to me sometimes. I remember one time when I was a kid, I was feeling lonely. I was crying in my room, and I told my mom I didn't have any friends. She laughed. "You got your sister. That's the only friend you will ever need," she said. I know what she meant by that. It was a nice notion about the importance of family. My parents were big on family. They were especially big on how sisters should treat each other, and how my sister and I should be best friends. We were, in a way. We liked each other, but I don't know if we were truly *best* friends until after the world fell away. I miss her a lot, now. I wish she was here with me. I wish she could see the house I live in, because she always wanted one just like it. I wish she could see the lake. I wish I could tell her about my boyfriend.

Boyfriend. That doesn't feel like it's the right word for what Twist is to me. It doesn't fit. He's not my husband, either. I don't know what to call him. I guess boyfriend and girlfriend are words you use to introduce someone you're seeing intimately to your other friends. *This is my boyfriend, Twist.* Without someone to hear that, it seems stupid. He's Twist. I'm Ren. That's what we are to each other. Me and him against the world. Literally.

We've been sharing the same bed for months. It's nice. I like having someone next to me at night. I know that neither of us sleeps particularly well. We both have bad dreams. There's a lot of tossing and turning in our bed at night. A lot of panic sweat and fear. The dreams—they're bad. Given what we've been through, I would not expect them to be anything but. We had to watch our families die. That's bound to mess up your neural synapses.

Twist never talks about his dreams, claims he doesn't remember them. I remember mine. I remember mine all too well. My dreams are always the same. Death. Sadness. Death. Sadness. Death. So much death. I watch my parents die all over. I watch my brother die again and again, powerless to do anything. My sister and I buried all three of them. Then, I watch my sister die. Watching her murder replays in my head often. I'll be out in the yard digging out weeds or planting something in the garden, and *bam!* I'll see her death in my mind. It just pops in without warning. I can never unsee it. I can be doing something innocuous like brushing my teeth, and my brain will say, *Your sister can never brush her teeth again.* And then I see her death in my mind. When it flashes in my brain, it usually plays in drawn-out slow-motion. It drives me crazy. I cannot seem to escape those images. I do not believe I ever will.

Twist doesn't seem to carry the sadness of loss like I do. Maybe he does, and he just is better than hiding it than I am. Maybe he made his peace with it. I haven't. I'm mad as hell about it all, and I can't get past it. The only time I'm sure he's sad like me is at night. He moans in his sleep sometimes, or he thrashes and it sounds like he's crying. When that happens, I try to press myself close to him, and he seems to relax. I like to be the Little Spoon in those moments. He encloses me in his arms while he sleeps, and it makes us both feel better. During the day, he's all smiles and jokes. At night, that's when I see the real him.

Jeez…this journal seems really pissy, doesn't it?

Now I have a whole new point of insecurity. I'll probably spend at least half an hour thinking about the hypothetical reactions of future civilizations reading this and trying to make scholarly assumptions about me, and about Twist. They'll love Twist, but that Renata girl—she was a real piece of work, just look at her whole basket of issues. That's just what I needed to round out my struggle in this world.

My personal bundle of neuroses aside, I have been spending most of my free time going through all the homes in the area for supplies. Twist doesn't like going into homes where people have died. He says it makes him feel like he's grave-robbing. I guess I get that, but I also get that those people are dead, and I'm still alive. I always try to think about these sorts of things by putting myself in their place. If I was dead, and someone who was still alive could benefit from my house, my supplies, or anything else I might have, let 'em. That's my motto. I was nearly done training to be a nurse when the Flu hit, only two weeks shy of graduating with a four-year degree. I know how valuable blood, plasma, bone marrow, and organs were. I had my donor card signed when I was sixteen. If I died, and my organs could help someone else, then by all means—take my organs. I don't see any difference between that and scavenging someone's home, regardless of the location of the bodies of the owners of the house.

I try to be respectful of the bodies. Most of them have devolved into a desiccated, near-mummified state. The insects had their way with the corpses initially, and then the liquids dried up and the bodies, subjected to that Texas heat and arid climate, became bricks of slowly decomposing carbon. I wrap the corpses in sheets as makeshift shrouds, and then Twist and I carry them out to a small handcart that we found. The cart is only about six feet long and four feet wide, but it has large wheels and a pair of joists off the front that make it easy to drag the cart along, or push it, if necessary. The handcart is one of those things that I didn't know we needed, but after we found it, I couldn't believe we didn't build it first thing.

Once the bodies were loaded on the cart, we carry them out to a large pit we found in a field a couple of miles away from the lake. At first, it seemed like such a long walk. Even in New York, a couple of miles was a bus ride or getting on the subway. Now, a couple miles is just the standard. We walk miles every day without thinking about it. I'm in pretty good shape because of it. I am vain enough to wish I had looked like I look now before the Flu.

The pit is about four or five feet deep. It looks like someone was trying to make an inverted pyramid. There are four wide sides that narrow to a point. The sides are lined with white, coral-like rocks for some reason. The bottom of the pit is dust. All around the pit is dirt and maybe a few blades of scrub grass, nothing that is going to burn. We line the bottom of the pit with scrub wood. We carry the bodies into the pit, lay them on the wood, slather them with jellied gasoline (burning is about the only thing gas is good for anymore), and add a few more pieces of scrub wood over them. Then, we light it. It's a strange funeral pyre, but it works. I always try to say a few words for the dead. I try to thank them for what they are unknowingly giving us. I try to tell them that everything they've given us will not go to waste. I hope they understand.

Once the bodies are taken care of, the house that remains is ours, so to speak. Twist lets me scavenge the homes because I'm way more methodical than he is, and he knows I like doing it. It might sound cruel or strange or sick in some way, but I love going through other people's homes. I feel like some sort of archaeologist entering an ancient tomb. All their secrets are there for the taking.

There are the normal, trivial things: food, for instance. You learn a lot about people by going through their pantries. Like, for instance, in one house, I found over fifty cans of Star Wars-branded chicken soup. Who can eat that much Jabba the Hutt-shaped pasta? I like going into really large, expensive homes and seeing how little food they have in their pantries, like they were sacrificing eating to be able to live in a nice house. You find out who likes Japanese food, who likes Tex-Mex, who likes Little Debbie snack cakes—you name it. And there are always houses filled with rice cakes, protein bars, and other cardboard-tasting health food—and those houses almost *always* have a hidden cache of candy bars, fatty snacks, and other tasty treats that give a big, metaphorical middle finger to the healthy eating. I wonder if that was one spouse's secret stash; I wonder if both spouses had weak moments. I like to envision the dynamics in the home based on their pantries.

I box up all the canned goods that Twist and I can eat, or that we can use to feed the chickens or the cows. I take the cat food, because our loyal house cat, Fester, likes his chow. It is a long and laborious process to clear the houses of food. Anything we're not going to eat, I open and spread in the woods for the wild creatures. We will eventually eat most of what we find, I reason—but there's no way I'm going to figure out what to do with sheets of dried *nori,* so those go to the squirrels.

After going through the kitchens and basements for food, I start a very careful, methodical investigation of the rest of the house. I go through all the furniture. Sometimes people hide things like wads of cash (*not like cash is worth anything now*) or books or magazines inside of ottomans or couches. I go through the magazines and books. Any books Twist or I might like to read comes back to the house with me. Any that we won't get put into plastic bags to keep them dry, just in case we ever need tinder for burning. I stack them in the living rooms of the homes so I know where they are if I ever need them. Anything that might be future-valuable gets stacked in the living rooms, actually. If I ever get to a point where I need something, I want it easily found again.

The bedrooms are always the best part of house-sacking. Clothes, of course, are valuable. I spend time going through the clothes and bagging them to keep them dry and vermin-free for the future. The clothes go to the living room. The linens may someday be necessary, but covers and blankets are blocky and hard to pack away, so I store them on high shelves in closets and hope for the best. Chances are, we will never need them all, so they're not that important. In the back of my head, I tell myself that someday I'm going to make a seriously kick-ass blanket fort. Who knows? Maybe that will happen.

The bedrooms are where you really get to learn about the people who lived in the homes, though. You find out their likes and dislikes. You find their secrets. Journals, porn, drugs, hidden caches of booze, stashes of Twinkies—all the guilty vices are in the bedrooms. If I find a handwritten journal, I will read it word-for-word. I will savor those words. It's the best window into people's lives. I've read journals that would break your heart—adultery, domestic violence, spouses thinking about leaving their longtime partner because the spark has gone out—you name, I've seen it. Without soap operas on TV, it's as close as I can come to watching telenovelas with my mom, again.

The bathrooms are what I save for last. I take great care to painstakingly bag all the toilet paper I can find. Empty wasteland or not, I *do not* want to live in a world without toilet paper. When Twist hitches the handcart to his bike and we go on runs to nearby little towns and houses farther away, he is under explicit orders to get all the toilet paper he finds. Spare no roll. Same thing with razors, deodorant, and feminine products. Twist sometimes jokingly calls me the Queen of Pads and Tampons. Screw him. He doesn't need that stuff once a month like I do. The house nearest to the nice two-story we chose to live in has become my "store." It's where I stash all the stuff we're going to need long-term like that. I want it nearby and available when necessary.

We don't have a standard water toilet anymore. That's a pipedream for when/if Twist gets the house up to running off of solar power and can tap the well pump. For now, we have to use a composting toilet because water is too valuable to waste like that. It's bad enough that I have to do my business in a bucket. I want to make it as easy as possible despite that. I do not want to have to do without toilet paper.

It is a strange existence, me spelunking houses for supplies, and Twist trying to turn himself into a gentleman farmer and hunter-gatherer supreme. What Twist and I have managed to carve out is not the life I had dreamed for myself, but it is a life. And the more I think about it, the more I think it's a *good* life. That's the most important thing.

In the house I scavenged this morning, I found the remnants of what was once a happy, young family. They did not die in the house, thankfully. Finding the dried corpses of infants is always difficult. Every time you see one of those babies, it takes a piece of you. You never get used to it. I doubt you ever could, and if you ever did, that meant that there was probably something deeply wrong and unsettled within you.

The house was clearly a starter home. A *very nice* starter home, but a starter home. There were still toys scattered around the living room, covered in a fine layer of dust. A large TV sat on a credenza, a pile of Muppets and Thomas the Tank Engine DVDs next to it. The posed, professionally-taken pictures on the wall showed a very nice, young family. The dad was holding a toddler. Dad was all toothy grin and polo shirt. The toddler looked like something straight out central casting, perfect round face and chubby cherub cheeks. A small boy, about four or five, was leaning against his mom's knee, a big, cheeky grin on his mug. He was dressed exactly like his dad, red polo and khakis. Mom was a beauty, with a perfect body despite pumping out two kids. She had expensive salon-maintained hair and a Texas beauty queen's sense of make-up and fashion. She wore the feminine version of the boys' outfits, a khaki skirt and a V-necked red sweater that displayed her impressive cleavage in a classy, yet *just* sexy enough to not be distasteful manner. They were the perfect suburban, wealthy young family. I was immediately jealous of them. I grew up poor, the middle child of two blue-collar, working immigrants. The only pictures we had laying around were school photos and the badly composed Polaroids that my auntie took anytime the family was gathered for a meal. Cell phone photos? Not until my sister and I got jobs as teens and paid for our own bottom-of-the-line Samsungs.

The house was a goldmine of useful things. The mother was just about my size. I'm short and petite. Finding clothes my size isn't always easy. The father was too short for me to outfit Twist in his slacks, but the shirts would work. The kitchen had a ton of nonperishable food that was miraculously free of vermin infestation. Once humanity died, the rats and mice went into overdrive. All the cardboard boxes in the world had at least teeth marks on them. If there was something remotely edible inside, you can bet your farm that a rat, raccoon, or a mouse took a run at it. Once, I went to make some instant potatoes. The box looked okay. The little press-in spout on the size was punctured, but only enough to maybe pass a peanut through. I ripped the top off and dumped the flakes into a pot of water. Two mouse corpses and a whole mess of mouse crap rolled out with it. The little demons can get *anywhere*. That instance scarred me for a while. Took me about two months to make or eat instant potatoes again.

The family had a bunch of nice tools in the garage, most of which were either electrical or required gas. That was a shame. I did find a lot of nails and some lumber. Twist and I had plans to start dismantling houses for the lumber in them when we needed construction material. Anything we could find that didn't require us ripping down drywall and knocking out two-by-fours from studding was a plus.

When I got to the bathrooms, I found a treasure trove of medications, creams, lotions, razors—you name it. Lots of sweet-smelling girly stuff. It was heavenly. There were massive jars of folic acid pills and prenatal vitamins. Apparently Mr. and Mrs. Perfect were not done pumping out spawn before the Flu hit. It looked like they were devotees of bulk warehouse shopping, and they had stocked up for the long haul. The master bath had a double-sink with a long cabinet beneath. Every square inch of that cabinet was stuffed with goodies that we would need. It was like Christmas to me.

I started throwing stuff in bags to take back to my store. It did not matter what it was, I knew it would eventually be useful. I loaded up. When I got to back of one of the drawers in the cabinet, I found a quartet of square boxes. I paused. Pregnancy tests. Time stopped. I stared at them for a long time.

I know what you're thinking: *Could she be pregnant?*

The answer to that is yes, probably.

I've known for a while, I guess. I just did not want to believe it. When a certain visitor failed to show up a while back, that was my first clue. Some pre-breakfast nausea was my second clue. And now my jeans and bras are starting to get tighter. Clue three. I had been denying the possibility too long. Now, I faced the possibility and just needed to confirm it.

I stood in the bathtub and peed on the stick. Then, I slapped the thing on the edge of the tub. I slid down against the wall of the master bath and sat in the dark room on the cool tile floor and waited. After an eternity, I flipped on my flashlight to read the results. In the little indicator window, there was a bright pink plus sign. I knew it was going to be there.

I ripped open a second box and took another test. After two minutes, another plus sign. *Damn.* I stared at the two sticks, both glowing with their pink positive symbols in the light of my Maglite, and I began to cry. Hard.

I do not want to be a mother. Not like this. Not here. Not now. I guess I had always wanted to be a mother one day, but that was before everyone in the world died. Now, it was just me and Twist against a constantly encroaching wilderness. There were not enough hours in the day to do what we needed to do as it was, and now the universe was going to throw a baby at us to complicate matters.

I should feel something other than profound sadness, but I didn't. There was no joy or excitement. There was just the soul-crushing reality of trying to have a baby in a world without hospitals, doctors, or epidurals. In a pre-modern medicine world, the infant mortality rate was somewhere between ten and twenty-five percent. One-fifth of all babies would die before they could be considered toddlers. Even as recently as 1960, the global infant mortality rate was still 20 percent. Almost 40 percent of children in 1800 would die before they turned five. How in the hell did Humanity even make it as far as it did?

My first great fear was that I would go through the struggle of carrying this thing inside me to just watch it die. My second great fear was that this thing inside me would kill *me*. Pre-modern medicine, the rate of women dying in childbirth was as high as eight to ten percent in some studies. The rate of women dying of infections post-birth climbed as high as 20 percent, depending on where the child was born and the financial status of the woman.

When I was studying nursing, when we studied birth, we

used to mock the Home Birthers. We used to make fun of them for thinking they knew better than modern medicine and their bold defiance of thinking they *probably* would not need a doctor, but now, as I faced a home birth of my own, I was in a panic. I did not want to do this by myself, and even more so—I didn't want Twist to have to act as obstetrician for this.

A curious and pragmatic mind will be asking me, *Hey, if you didn't want kids, why didn't you use protection? Surely there are still condoms and other forms of birth control available to you.* And those curious minds will be correct. We *were* trying to be careful. We were using condoms. However, those curious minds also need to be willing to understand that we are young and stupid, and things happen. If I reconstruct the timeline in my head, I could even hazard a guess at precisely *when* it happened: a warm, romantic night, away from the house, atop a lovely hill, watching a sunset, a shimmering lake laid out before us, a blanket picnic, too much wine, some flirting, some kissing, and kissing turned into groping, and…yeah.

In the dark of the bathroom, I cried until I couldn't cry anymore. A pregnancy should be a happy thing. My mother and my sister should be around to rejoice in this event. My dad should be there. God, he wanted to be a granddad in the *worst* way. He kept bugging my older sister about settling down and giving him a little someone he could take to Mets games. My dad would have been over-the-friggin'-moon. Thinking about how he would have reacted only made this worse. How would I explain my dad and how great he was to this kid? This child would never know his grandparents, aunts, or uncle. I don't even have pictures of them. I left all the crappy Polaroids back in Brooklyn. My sadness turned to sudden, unexplainable, violent rage. I sprinted downstairs to the expensive, framed family pictures on the wall, ripped them from their hooks, and hurled them at the far wall, smashing the glass. So much fear. So much rage. So much…uncertainty. That picture-family did not deserve the way they were treated, but then again, I don't think I deserved to have a baby in a world where that baby would never have any friends his or her own age.

Oh, Twist…what have we done?

I collapsed on the couch in a petulant huff. Dust clouds rose up around me and made my sinuses itch. I started crying again. I started trying to reassure myself that everything would be okay.

I remembered watching a documentary in one of my high school Social Studies classes. It showed a woman in rural Asia working in a rice paddy. She stopped work midmorning, went back to her family hut, pumped out a baby, fed it from her breast, wrapped it in towels, swaddled it to her body with a sling, and then made dinner for her family who were still working in the field. Life went on. There were still chores to do. If she could do it, I certainly could. I thought about Caroline Ingalls giving birth to Carrie in a remote log cabin on the vast and empty Kansas plains. If she could do it, so could I. Women have been pumping out anklebiters without so much as a doctor's nod for *millennia!* I told myself, I will be fine.

I kept repeating that like a mantra. *You will be fine. You will be fine. You will be fine.*

You know what they say—if you lie to yourself long enough, maybe you'll start to believe it.

I ran my hand over my stomach. I wasn't showing yet, but I could tell my stomach was starting to get bigger. I still had some abdominal muscle definition. I still *looked* like I wasn't pregnant, but it was getting there. I had to be almost three months along at this point. My hips were getting a little wider. My thighs were a little bigger. At the beginning of this journal, I lamented about how we don't really keep track of time. That is now a sticking point for me. I wish I *had* kept better track. I wish I knew *exactly* how long I was. I wish I knew what the timeline would be. I tried to remind myself again that women, for centuries, kept track of this sort of stuff through general terms. It was now spring. This child would show up in mid-to-late fall. October-*ish*, most likely. That was a long time to go. It seemed like an eternity.

I didn't want to tell Twist, but I knew that telling him was the next logical step, the only step, really. He needed to know. He deserved to know. How would he react? Would he be happy or sad? Anticipating his reaction scared me, a little.

In my neighborhood, I saw girls lose their boyfriends because they got knocked up. It happened so often, it became a cause for celebration when their guys actually stuck around and participated in the kid's life. It happened to a good friend of mine from high school. Isadora got knocked up, told Carlo, and at first he acted happy. Then, within a month, he was gone. He ran off to Queens, hooked up with some broad there. Isa gave birth to a happy, healthy baby boy a few months later, and spent most of her free time trying to get Carlo to pony up child support or come visit his son. Twist did not strike me as the type who would run off, and given our situation, where could he go? It's not like there are a lot of other options out there for him. But, still. It's not like we planned this. It's not like we're married. It's not like we'd be together, save for the highly improbable chain of circumstances that somehow put us on intersecting paths. A lot of really far-out stars had to align for us to end up in Texas trying to build a farm together. I just worried about how this would change him.

Change *us*.

I did not want us to change. I liked where we were, as people and as a couple. I liked the life we were building. A baby was going to be a whole new wrinkle in that dynamic, and I was not sure it would work.

I lazed around that house for most of the afternoon. When

I got hungry *(which was frequently)*, I demolished bag after bag of Goldfish crackers. Thanks, bulk warehouse club. I drank cans of LaCroix sparkling water because the woman had a small vault filled with it in the pantry. I stared blankly out the window. I cried a lot more. And I worried.

I knew that Twist was probably back at the farm. Maybe he'd had some luck with hunting. Thinking about a dinner that didn't taste like processed mac'n'cheese and saltines made my stomach growl. Thinking about some sort of fresh meat cooked over a fire made me *really* hungry. I put off facing the music long enough; I had to go back.

Courage, girl. Don't worry. You and Twist will get through this together.

I repeated my mantra: *You will be fine. You will be fine. You will be fine.*

I gathered a bag of supplies I could carry back to my store. I grabbed the pregnancy tests. I took a deep breath, steeled myself for the walk back to the farm, and I started hiking. I stopped. Went back into the house, searched the bookshelves, and found the dog-eared copy of *What to Expect When You're Expecting* that I just knew would be there, and put that in the bag, too. I was going to need that book.

The entire way back to the house, I worried more with each step. My legs turned to jelly. My stomach filled with butterflies. I felt like my bladder was going to release.

When I turned the corner around the edge of the house and saw our great yard, Twist was there. He looked so tall and handsome. He was shirtless, preparing some sort of meat over the fire. An enticing scent, like roasted pork, hung over the yard. At that moment, I was almost knocked over by a sudden, passionate wave of love for him. Fester, our large black-and-white house cat was roaming around by the fire, looking for scraps. Several of our chickens were hunting insects in the grass. I could see Thing 1 and Thing 2 watching Twist over the fence of their paddock.

Everything was so perfect…and yet, it wasn't. I could not

shake the feeling that we had done something very wrong. How stupid is that? The most natural thing in the world, to me, was somehow wrong? I could not shake the feeling that my being pregnant was a mistake. I kept feeling like Twist was going to run or hate me or…or, I don't know what. I was sick to my core and miserable anticipating his reaction. And I have no idea what it says about me that I was certain he was going to have a negative reaction. Clearly, I have some serious emotional baggage rattling around in my brain that I have yet to unpack.

I dropped the bag of stuff I was carrying. My fingers squeezed hard on the pregnancy tests I carried. Twist heard the sound of the bag hitting the ground, but he didn't turn around. He had a big knife in his hand and was concentrating on cutting meat. "Hey, babe," he said. "Your man has brought back meat! I have successfully hunted! Have you ever had javelina?"

I didn't answer. I had no idea what a javelina was. It smelled incredible, though. That was more than enough to set my mouth to watering. If javelina tasted as good as it smelled, I was willing to eat every javelina that dared cross my path.

You will be fine. You will be fine. You will be fine.

"Hey, Twist…" I started to say. The words caught in my throat. I felt like I was choking. I coughed.

Twist stopped cutting and turned to glance at me over his shoulder. "You okay, babe?" He stopped. He immediately looked worried. "Ren? What's wrong?"

I guess my face betrayed me. I could only imagine how blotchy I looked, and I knew my eyes were red from crying most of the afternoon. All it took was the genuinely sincere look of concern on his face to set off my waterworks again. I started crying hard. Sobs wracked through my chest and felt like they were going to break my ribs. My legs gave out, and I fell to my knees, then fell over on my side in the grass. I did not want to tell him. I did not want to do this. I wished I wasn't pregnant. I wished for that harder than I ever wished for anything in my life, but like all my other wishes, it would go unanswered.

Twist's eyes went wide. "Are you hurt? What happened?" He dropped his knife and started looking for a towel to wipe off the blood on his hands.

I tried to tell him I wasn't hurt, but I couldn't form words. Instead, I just sat up and lifted my hand to show him the two pregnancy tests.

Twist was frozen in place. It took a moment, but he slowly recognized what I was holding. He looked from the tests, to me, and back to the tests. Then, he threw his head back and began to laugh.

CHAPTER THREE

Victor

I can't say I had *always* imagined this moment in my life, but I had done it a couple of times. When I was younger and the Internet still existed, I used to indulge in the secret guilty pleasure of watching YouTube videos of women revealing pregnancies to their partners or parents. Those videos always seemed like the cure for the negativity and pessimism of the world. The unfettered joy of those people was a sweet, brief elixir to everything that was wrong in society. When I wasn't tired at night, I would watch them for a while, get a little teary-eyed, and then go to sleep. It was comforting. I liked to imagine that one day, I would have a wife who would do some sort of elaborate pregnancy reveal to me, and I wondered how I would react. Would I be happy? Would I cry? Would I be stunned by disbelief?

Nope. I laughed.

I laughed *hard*, too.

I can't explain it. It just seemed to be so surreal. It seemed impossible. As far as my brain was concerned, what Ren had just done was so amazing and unlikely that it was on the same level as farce. Monty Python themselves could have just jumped out from the corner of the house and screamed *"Nobody expects the Spanish Inquisition!"* It would have been no less strange and hilarious to me.

Ren looked a miserable sight at that moment, and the juxtaposition of her tiny frame holding out those tests, fat tears streaming down her face, and knowing what those tests meant just broke my brain. At that moment, I had never laughed harder. My laughter stunned Ren. She stopped crying and her face went slack. She looked confused. Her confusion only made me laugh harder.

I dropped to my knees in front of her. My stomach hurt from laughing. My cheeks hurt. Ren's face slowly lost the look of confusion and she smiled. I knew she didn't want to smile, so the fact that she had to only made it funnier. I threw my arms around her, still laughing, and in seconds, we were both howling with laughter. Maybe it wasn't a YouTube-worthy pregnancy reveal, but I would not have traded it for anything.

I fell backward, dragging Ren on top of me. I held her there while I let the final peals of laughter make their way out of my body.

Ren punched my shoulder playfully. "Jerk. And here I thought you'd be mad."

"Mad? How could I be mad?"

Ren shrugged. "I just...I don't know. I'm stupid. Shut up."

Something in the tone of her voice chased the final laughs out of my chest. We lay in the grass for a long moment. Her face pressed into my chest. I stroked her hair. I felt her breathing. "Are you okay?"

She shrugged again. "Yeah. No. I don't know." She pushed herself up and straddled me, sitting on my stomach. "Twist, I'm pregnant."

"Who's the father?"

"Really, smartass? That's the card you want to play right now?" She smiled and thumped my sternum with her fist. The smile was quickly chased from her face, though. She swallowed hard. "I'm scared."

The smile ran from my face, too. "Me, too. It's not like this isn't perfectly natural, though. Animals get pregnant. They give birth. It's the way of the world."

"I know. It's just...there should be a hospital, doctors, you know."

"Women for centuries—" I started.

She cut me off. "I know what women have been doing. I've been thinking about it for weeks. That does not mean I want to have to do it that same way. I wanted every drug they could give me. I wanted to go to sleep and wake up with a doctor handing me a baby and saying, 'Congrats! It's a boy!' I am not going to get any of that."

"Women—" I started again.

Ren's eyes narrowed. "If you try to tell me about what women have done again, I'm going to punch you right in the beak. I *know* what they did, fool! I am a woman! I was almost a nurse. This is not new knowledge. I'm not a rube. I don't care what *they* did. This is *me* we're talking about. Not them."

I smelled something burning at that moment. The javelina. I rolled Ren off me. "C'mon. We'll eat something and talk. You'll feel better after you eat." I helped her to her feet.

"You have no idea. What is it I'm about to eat all of, leaving you nothing, anyhow?"

We sat in the chairs near the fire while I roasted hunks of javelina over the fire. The mesquite wood smoke flavored the meat well, and we added a little barbecue sauce to the finished product. I told Ren about the hunt, and what javelinas were. We both agreed that they were tasty. It was a pork-like meat, but a touch more gamy, as wild game is apt to be, I'm told by all the hunting articles I've read. It would never hit the top three in best meats I've eaten, but given that I hunted it myself and it was the first fresh meat we had in ages, it tasted far better than it probably should have.

Ren demolished it. She loaded her plate and ate as much as she could hold. "I get to eat and get fat now. That's the rules."

I was not about to argue with a pregnant woman about the rules. Instead, when I finished eating, I tossed a few pieces of scraps to Fester, and then reclined in my seat, shifting to look at Ren. "I am happy about this," I said. "A few months ago, I guess I made up my mind that I'd never be a father. I guess I assumed it was out of the realm of possibility."

"I did not want to get pregnant." Ren spat a piece of gristle into the fire. "I didn't want this to happen, Twist."

"And now that it has?"

She shook her head. "I don't know. I'm not sure. I'm still processing it, I guess."

"Is any part of you happy?"

Ren thought about this and conceded it with a nod of her head. "Yes. Sort of. I can't help but think that my sister should be here. My mom should be here, too. I can't share this with them and it hurts me, you know?"

"I understand." I let silence descend after that. What could I say? We were both trying to move on, to forge ahead in the world and let the past be the past, but you never stop grieving. You just figure out a way to function while grieving. Moments of joy like this make the loss and separation that much more painful.

"I'm scared, too." Ren reached out and put one of her hands on mine. "What if…something goes wrong?"

"We deal with it."

"How?"

I shrugged. "As best we can. We've dealt with everything else, so far. We'll figure it out."

"That's not comforting."

"It's all I've got right now."

Ren was silent again. After a few minutes of staring into the fire, she started to laugh. "My cousin Jaime got married a few months before the Flu. Of course, my Auntie Sofia wanted to know when they were going to get to baby-making. Jaime's wife was in law school. She was a very prim, proper upstate white chick, right? She goes, 'Oh, I don't think I want to bring a baby into the world, things being what they are.' My Auntie looks at her like she'd just grown an extra head. She says, '*Chica*, I was born in a goddamned *hut*. I want to be an *abuela*!"

"People were still getting pregnant while bombs were being dropped on London in World War II," I said. "I guess the lights-out orders made them feel romantic. Keep calm and carry on, indeed."

"I guess we can't stop the natural order, no matter how hard the natural order tried to stop us."

I covered her hand with my other hand. "We will be fine," I said.

"That's what I've been trying to tell myself. How can we be sure?"

"How can we be sure a tornado won't drop out of the sky and kill both of us tonight while we sleep?"

Ren stuck out her tongue at me. "*Touché.*"

"They used to say we could only be sure of death and taxes. Taxes don't exist anymore, so we only have to worry about death now. Life is fifty percent easier than it used to be, if you use that metric."

"We're going to have a baby, Twist. A baby in this world. What kind of future can it have?"

"Whatever future it wants to have. We will help it as best we can, and it can figure out the rest on its own, just like every other person has since time began."

"We sound stupid calling it 'It.' Is this a baby or a demonic clown?"

"Hey, it can be both if it wants."

"*He,*" Ren corrected me. "It's a boy." She set her plate down and put her hands on her stomach. "A strong baby boy."

"How can you tell?"

"I'm Latin, and I'm going to be a mother. Latinas always know these things."

"A boy it is, then."

We lapsed into a long silence. The sun set, and we stared into the dancing flames of the fire pit. The night was warm, but not so warm that the fire was unwelcome. Fester lounged in the grass between us, tail twitching. We held hands, both of us trying to channel strength from the other.

I was scared, but this was a different kind of fear than anything I'd known in the last two years. It used to be that I was scared of death, or loneliness, or Bigfoot, but those were fears I could carry on my own shoulders. That was all on me, no one else. When Ren came into my life, my fear spread to blanket her, too. Now, I worried about her as much as I worried about myself—no, I worried about her more than myself. However, she was a woman grown. She could handle herself. My mistakes need not hurt her. As I sat and contemplated a new life, I realized that my decisions, my successes and failures, would carry far more weight than they had in the past. If I fail to hunt, that child starves. If I fail to gather wood, that child will be cold. If I fail anything, that child will carry some of whatever the fallout of that failure would be. That thought froze my guts. I wasn't prepared for that sort of burden.

"We will call him Victor," Ren said.

"Why Victor?"

"My father's name was Victor."

It was a good name. Simple and strong. "Victor it is, then." I liked the implications of the name. Victor, victory—Ren and I survived, and we continue to survive. We beat the Flu. We won. The child will be a fighter, too. It was a good name, a fitting name.

She squeezed my hand. In that squeeze, I found warmth that melted away much of the fear. I was going to be a father.

Ren fell asleep easily, curled into a small ball next to me. I did not. I laid in bed for two or three hours, restless, before I eased myself out from under the covers. I threw on some shorts and my favorite hooded sweatshirt. I walked downstairs, slipped out the door to the yard, and walked barefoot through the damp grass to the road in front of the house. The day's heat was still being held by the asphalt, and it felt good on my feet. I stood in the middle of the road and stared at the moon.

I thought about how young I was. I know that people have successfully parented much younger than I, however that was of little comfort to me. That was them; I'm me. I have no idea how to be a dad. I had a good dad, don't get me wrong. The template is there. I just have never given serious thought to how to raise a kid, especially in this post-human world. What is this kid going to do? What is he going to be? I started getting overwhelmed with emotions that I'd never experienced before and didn't know how to process any of them. It was too strange, too new. I barely know what I'm doing. I can barely keep myself alive, let alone Ren, and now a *baby*!

Part of me was delighted by the prospect of being a father. Part of me wanted it a lot, far more than I thought I did. The other part of me had no idea what to expect. It was that part of me where all the creeping fear began to accumulate. Ren might have been eating for two, but I was worrying for three. I wondered if that was typical for new fathers-to-be. Something told me that it probably was.

After dinner, Ren and I spent most of the night talking around the fire. We discussed things we would need: diapers, formula, supplies, clothes—stuff like that. And we discussed stuff we would need for the actual delivery—most importantly, I'd need a book that explained *how* to deliver a baby at home. I'd have to go to a library and see what I could find. We talked about nutritional needs. Ren would need a lot of vegetables and fruits. She would need a steady supply of iron. She wasn't craving pickles, but she did say she would be willing to fight a bear for a box of Little Debbie Swiss Cake Rolls (*and who could blame her?*), so I suppose I will have to find some of them *toot suite*.

My stomach started to get fluttery. Nerves. Worry. A lot of worry. Too much worry, perhaps. I started thinking about my own mortality. When the Flu first hit, I thought about checking out of the planet manually, on my own terms. I decided against it, if for no other reason than I was still living despite the world trying to make sure I wasn't. I figured it was a good reason to spite the planet. When I met Ren, she gave me a simple reason for living: I loved her, and I wanted to be around her. Now, the idea of a baby, of a small, dependent life that not only needed me to live, but to provide knowledge, leadership, love, and direction. That life would need to be fed and nurtured. It would need to be taught to survive. How in the hell could I teach a baby to survive when I've only been winging it, myself? And what if the inevitable happened and I died? What then? What if Ren predeceased me, and then I passed away from illness, rogue peccary attack, or accident? Anything was possible. What would happen to that baby? What if that baby was a toddler or a child when I died? What then? And how would I educate that baby? I never even graduated from high school!

I sank down to the road and cried. I didn't know what I was doing, and I did not feel like I ever would. I sure as hell was not prepared to raise a child in this world. At that moment, I wanted my mom. Seems silly to say that, but it's true. I wanted to go to her and get her advice. She was only twenty-two when she had me. Granted, my birth was not all that unusual. She and my dad were married, and my dad had recently passed the CPA exams, so they were going to be alright. But, I wanted to hear her voice. I wanted to hear her excitement for this baby. I wanted her to tell me what to do and how to handle it.

I laid in the road a long time. I spent hours watching stars and trying to talk myself into being a parent. I fell back to using logic, as I so often have. *Put it perspective*, my dad used to say. So, I did. I was not going to be the first person on the planet to have to raise a child without a lot of help. I was not going to be the first person to have to deliver his own baby. I was not going to be the first person to raise a child without basic utilities, television, and public schools. The more I put things in perspective, the better I felt about the situation. I started to think about the positives. I tried to picture the baby Ren and I would make. Would it look like her, or like me? I hoped it would have her nose, at least. I never liked my nose; I always thought it looked too big for my face. I started thinking about teaching my future son to hunt, and to harvest. I thought about him playing with kittens in the barn, or chasing chickens around the yard. This kid would be the first American child in a couple of generations to be raised by firelight and books instead of television. I reminded myself that this kid would never know the world as it was before, so he would only know the world as it was now. I wasn't scared of the world before the Flu, so he would not be scared of the post-Flu world. He would be a hunter and gatherer from birth. He would raise his own animals. I would teach him to read and farm and hunt, and then books and experience would have to teach him the rest.

Maybe having a kid wouldn't be so bad.

I started to get excited about it, actually. I started to *want* to be a dad. The desire for a child started like a spark, but quickly caught flame. I suddenly really wanted to be a father. I wanted it more than anything else, at that moment. After all, that's the whole point, right? Perpetuate the species. Keep humanity alive. I was going to do my part.

But, first…

CHAPTER FOUR

For Better or Worse

I woke with a start. Something was wrong. The bed was empty. That, in and of itself, was not unusual. Twist generally slept a lot less than I did, especially since I became an incubator. He usually eased himself out of bed around dawn and started on his day. Most days I slept until he had breakfast ready. He was a morning person. I was not. However, the bed being empty made all the fears of him running away a sudden reality. For a split second, I was back in my old neighborhood disappointing my parents by getting knocked up with the father being little more than a sperm donor dodging out when it came time to pay the piper. I felt shame well up inside me. Tears smarted at the corner of my eyes. *C'mon, Ren—get it together.* Stupid hormones.

It was dark, still the middle of the night. Where was Twist? I walked through the house. He was nowhere to be found. He was not in the shack we'd built to house our composting toilet, either. *(Believe me, having an outhouse is not the height of glamorous, but needs dictate what needs must.)* When I didn't find him in the barn, I got really scared. And angry. I wanted to hurt him at that second, which is stupid. I *know* Twist. He's kind. He's got a good heart. He wouldn't run. But, the pregnancy hormones are silly. They make you overreact. Every insecurity I had suddenly flooded my brain. I ran back to our bedroom and cried again. Partly because of hormones, and partly because of fear.

After the Flu hit, I made peace with the world being the way it was. I spent my days crawling through people's apartments in New York for food, books, and supplies. I figured that was going to be what my life was until I died, be it from accident, old age, or personal choice. The idea of being a mother never, ever occurred to me during that first year. It seemed silly to think about being someone's parent in a world that was barely equipped to keep me alive.

When I met Twist, I saw a better option for life. He was going south, and that sounded better than sticking around New York for another stupid winter. He had an RV, a cat, and supplies. He was clearly better at this whole survival thing than I was, and he was willing to share, to help me. It made sense for me to hitch my wagon to his. The idea of being a mother crept into my head then, briefly. A fleeting image. Me and him, the last two people on Earth, the whole "Adam and Eve" thing was there. How could it not be? But, I decided quickly that I did not want a baby, not because I didn't like Twist, but because it would be asking too much of that child. Maybe the Flu did exactly what it was supposed to do, right? Maybe it was time for humanity to end, and who was I to buck Nature? Humankind was supposed to end, and I was content to be a mistake in the Grand Plan, but that mistake should end with me.

I guess Nature had other plans.

I'm scared. I suppose I can say that. I'm terrified. I did not want this baby, but now that I know for certain that it's there, I can't imagine *not* wanting it. I don't want it for Twist's sake, or Nature's Plans, or even for the good of Humanity—I want it because of some primordial maternal instinct that I didn't even know I had. As I lay in that empty bed, my pessimistic brain trying to convince me that Twist had run off rather than be my baby's father, I vowed to have that baby regardless of anything else. Nothing would prevent me from having this kid and raising him. I would teach him whatever I could, and he would have to learn the rest on his own. I didn't need Twist, my parents, my sister—I would do this. Me. Me alone.

I went back to sleep, but it was an uneasy sleep, and eventually the noise of the birds in the trees around the house roused me out of bed at dawn. I threw a hand over to Twist's side of the bed. It was cold. He had not slept there. I tried to reassure myself, tell myself that he was just nervous or excited and was somewhere doing chores or something.

I dressed, preparing for another day of house scavenging, or maybe I'd take my bike to look for fruit trees. Fresh peaches sounded good. Apples sounded even better. I wished there were banana trees around here. I could use the potassium. I could also work in the garden. We had a nice plot of plants coming up, corn and potatoes, some assorted veggies. There was always plenty to do on the farm. And it would never end. I would do it all by myself, if I had to.

I grabbed breakfast. We had a large store of Pop-Tarts and dried oatmeal. I went with Pop-Tarts because they were as good cold as they were hot. I slipped on my shoes and went outside, hoping to see Twist at the fire. He wasn't. The embers were not even stoked. Wherever he was, it wasn't on the property. Fine. Screw 'em. I don't need him anyway. I refused to cry.

You're being stupid, girl, I told myself. Where would he even go? He was around. Knowing Twist, he was off trying to figure out some grand scheme for the future, or maybe he remembered something in a house nearby that he absolutely needed to have at that moment. He wasn't exactly impulsive, but when he got one of his silly notions, he would have to follow it through. Still, all the reassuring in the world did not make me feel better.

I ate my Pop-Tarts and drank a large glass of bottled water. Twist was working on getting a filtering system up and running so we could harvest lake water and purify it for our needs, but until then, we had a whole bedroom full of bottled water that we'd been hording for months. Then, I gathered up my little canvas knapsack of supplies, added some food, and prepared to go hike down the road to go through another house. I was almost out of the yard before I remembered the pills. I had to go back and take some of Mrs. Perfect's prenatal vitamins and some of that folic acid. This was to be the new normal for me. Take the pills. Make sure the baby would be healthy. I had my mission.

When I walked back out to the yard, Twist was riding up the little driveway on his mountain bike. I froze. Half of my pregnancy-addled brain fully expected never to see him again, and the other half wanted to take him right there on the concrete. It is a wild ride in the raging river that is my emotions, let me tell you.

He ditched his bike by stepping over the bar, stepping off the pedal smooth as silk, and letting the bike ghost-ride itself into the grass. It was a cool move, I admit.

"Where have you been?" There was more vitriol in my voice than I wanted it to have, but I couldn't help it. "I was—" I choked off the sentence. He didn't need to know I was worried.

"I couldn't sleep."

"Yeah, I noticed."

Twisted slipped his backpack off his shoulders. "Ren, I've been thinking—"

"You don't have to think." The words snapped out of my mouth before I could stop them. "You don't have to stay. I will raise this kid on my own." Twist looked like I had just slapped him. I immediately felt bad and regretted spouting off like an insecure fool. "I'm sorry. I just...I'm not myself right now."

Undaunted, Twist tried again. "I said that I was thinking

last night. I thought a lot about being a dad. And I think…I think this is a great thing. I'm really, really happy that you're…that we…well, you know." He nodded toward my stomach.

I almost cried again. God, I hated my emotions going from coast-to-coast like this. I hated what the surges were doing to me. I wanted to be stronger. I did not want to give into those feelings. There was a time and a place, and this was neither. *Fight it, Ren.* I swallowed hard and cleared my throat. "Me, too."

"I just…I want to do this right. I want to be a good dad."

"You will be."

Twist fumbled in his backpack. "No, I mean, if we're going to do this, then let's do it all the way." He pulled out a small, square velvet box. A ring box. He popped the top of the box to reveal a large diamond ring. He dropped to a knee in front of me in the driveway. "Renata Lameda, mother of my future child, would you marry me?"

Honestly, if I had known pregnancy was going to make me cry this much, I would have reconsidered the whole deal.

It was a stupid gesture. Marriage was a societal convention, and we were two people without a society. Who would marry us? And a ring? Wholly impractical and ridiculous for a woman who was going to have to labor with her hands a lot. I should have told him he was being stupid, but I was overjoyed at the prospect of being a wife before I was a mother. I know it's silly to think about that in a wasteland without rules, but I was raised in a strict Catholic household and my parents beat marriage into my head since I was a fetus. I held out my hand and let him slip the ring onto my finger.

"I had to ride to that little town a few miles away to get the ring. I hope you like it. I think it's the right size." Twist smiled at me with that crooked smile of his.

"It's perfect."

"Then, let's get married."

I laughed. "Where? The nearest church is miles away, and besides, I haven't had time to figure out who to invite."

Twist pointed to the hill overlooking the lake. "There. Let's do it now."

I shook my head. "No. The ring is good enough. Knowing that you want to be married is good enough."

Twist would not be dissuaded. He grabbed my hand and started walking, dragging me along with him. "No. This is necessary."

"I look like crap." My protests fell on deaf ears.

"You look beautiful. You *are* beautiful."

We walked to the top of the hill. Twist picked a bouquet of wildflowers as we walked, passing them to me when we got to the top. He took my hands in his. He shouted out to the empty world around us, "Dearly beloved, we are gathered here today to join these two people in matrimony. If anyone has any objections, speak now or forever hold your peace."

He paused, listening to the easy morning wind and the sound of the ducks on the water. He shrugged and winked at me. "Huh. I was sure someone would speak up."

"Me, too," I said. "Given how many of our exes are in the audience, you'd think someone would want to break this up."

Twist smiled. "Renata Maria Lameda, I, Barnabas James Stickler, do hereby solemnly swear to take you as my wife, for better or for worse, in sickness, health, and pregnancy, until death do we part. Do you, Renata Maria Lameda, take me, Barnabas James Stickler, as your husband, for better or for worse, in sickness, health, and farming, until death do we part?"

There was something about the earnestness in his face, the smile, and the eyes—there was something about that moment in time, and the silence around us that, if I had not already loved him, would have remedied that situation. I fell in love with him all over again. "I do."

"Then, by the authority of the big Texas sky overhead, and the farm we are building, I declare us husband and wife. What the Flu has joined, let no man tear asunder. Now I get to kiss the bride."

I stopped him. "Shouldn't I have the authority to marry us? After all, I'm the President of the United States." Last fall, when he and I were in Washington D.C., he swore me in as president in the Oval Office of the White House.

"Good point," he agreed. "You should do the honors, Madam President."

I tossed the wildflowers over my shoulders and pressed myself against him. "Kiss me, First Husband."

And he did.

For that moment, the world was a perfect place again.

The reality of being a new wife and mother in a world where we were all alone was not lost on me. I knew that I would not get a lot of the benefits that most pregnant women get in first world, developed countries. No putting my feet up and relaxing while the world revolves around me. I would have to do my fair share around the farm, no matter how house-like my belly became. I could not expect Twist to work himself to the bone, dawn-to-dusk, with me lazing about just because I had a bellyful of baby. Even if I had to do less work, there would always be things I could do. I kept the images of all the strong, tough pioneer women who worked in the fields and the woods alongside their husbands and still made three meals a day for their families, no matter how pregnant they were. I was young, strong, and healthy. There was no reason I could not emulate those women. They would be my role models. If Caroline Ingalls could do it, I could, too.

I also knew that I was not going to get any of the perks that came with being pregnant. Back in the old neighborhood, when a young wife got pregnant, it was *always* a big deal. No one in my neighborhood was rich, but we all got by. When a young wife first announced her pregnancy, there was always a party with big cakes and lots of celebrating. Everyone asked how she was. All the old *abuelas* would come up and rub her belly and make wishes for her to have a strong, healthy son. And then, when she was closer to her due date, there was always a big baby shower. And when the baby came home from the hospital, everyone would turn out with gifts and casseroles and offers to babysit. It was really nice. I was going to get none of that, and it made me a little sad. I knew I couldn't dwell on that, though. I was going to have my own share of trials and tribulations on this journey, and to get depressed about the things I couldn't control would waste too much time.

At least I was given the gift of Twist's constant attentions. He went to another level of attentiveness. He would check on me often, make sure I was feeling okay. He would bring me water during the day and make sure I was hydrated. He somehow kept his concern and attentions attuned to the precise volume of visits where I felt cared for, but not annoyed.

What can I say? I married a winner.

With the acceptance of the situation, I started allowing myself the privilege of looking forward to it. At three months, the thing in my womb was basically a salamander with a human face. It looks human, according to the pregnancy books, but it at the same time, it's not really human. It's just a blob floating in fluid. I started to wonder what he would look like. I saw myself carrying a baby in one of those baby backpacks while I worked around the farm. I saw a toddler following me around the farm, or maybe I was pulling him in a wagon.

Then, I started thinking about everything we would need. I sat down at the table in our kitchen and started penning out a list. The more I thought, the more extensive the list became. The more extensive the list became, the more I started to stress about it. The more I started to stress about it, the more I started to pick apart the minute details about it. The more I started to pick apart the details, the more I started seeing every possible worst-case scenario. Then, one morning a few days after our wedding, I was out gathering eggs from the chicken coop. I picked one up, and while moving to transfer it to the bowl I used to carry them to the house, I lost my grip on the stupid thing, and it fell and shattered on the floor, a slimy, yolky mess. Right then and there, I started crying. I sank to my knees on the gross coop floor and wept. What was I doing? I wasn't a mother. I couldn't even hold an egg! What was I going to do with a baby? What if I dropped him? What if he got sick? What if I got sick and couldn't take care of him? A million *What Ifs...* popped into my head at that moment.

It made me mad that I was that emotional about it, too. I was never one of those girls that cried. I never threw fits, especially after my sister died, and I was left alone in this world. I just dealt with what came, accepted it as it was, and tried to figure out how to do things better afterward. This, though—the gravity of it, the weight on my shoulders, the fear, the uncertainty, the potential for disaster or failure—it was all too much.

Twist was out doing god-knows-what god-knows-where, and I was thankful for that. I didn't want him seeing me having a breakdown. The last thing I needed was for him to worry more about me. Don't get me wrong, I liked knowing he cared, but I also liked knowing that I was slightly older than he was, and more experienced, and I wanted to maintain that aura as long as I could.

I allowed myself the therapy of a good cry, and then I cleaned up the egg, finished gathering eggs, and went back inside to finish my list. At the top of the list, I printed the words: Operation Baby. It made it feel official, like it was a military plan. I was going to do this. I would make it happen. *You will be fine.* I repeated my mantra over and over in my head. *You will be fine. You will be fine.* With my list in my pocket, I gathered up my knapsack of supplies and set off for a new house to scavenge.

CHAPTER FIVE

A Necessary Horse

It feels strange. After Ren's announcement and our hasty marriage, life just continued to roll on, an eternal ticking clock. There was no honeymoon for us *(where would we even go?)* and there were too many things that needed to be done around the farm *(because maintenance was a never-ending task)*, so we simply kissed, became husband and wife, and told each other we'd celebrate at dusk. Then, it was business as usual.

I spent the rest of the day digging post holes to expand a paddock from the barn for the potential addition of a horse. Horses needed a lot of space, and expanding the paddock was mindless, repetitive work. I had never used a post hole digger before hitting Texas. It's a strange sort of shovel with two sides, each attached to a long handle with a hinge in the middle of them. You stomp the metal end into the earth, scissor apart the handles, and lift out the dirt. It takes a long time to dig out a fence post hole to a sufficient depth for planting a post. Then, you move eight or ten feet down the line and repeat. This is a horrible task on the best of days. Under a hot Texas sun, it was a miserable task. I slathered sunscreen on my neck and face, wore a wide-brimmed jungle hat to keep off the sun, and sweated profusely through my long-sleeved shirt and jeans.

At one point, I was in something of a daze. I was probably a little dehydrated and definitely tired given how little I had slept the night before. I took a step back from my digging and heard the distinct sound of a maraca being shaken. Given that I was certain there were no bands of roaming Mariachi, I froze. A new, cold, fear-based sweat broke out on my body. I had not been in Texas very long, but I knew the early warning device of a rattlesnake when I heard it. I craned my head around and saw a long, healthy Diamondback curled into strike position. The rattle at the end of its tail was long and as thick around as my thumb. This was a fully grown snake. Even with bottles of antivenin back at the house, a snake bite would put a serious crimp in my style. I knew that snakes were movement hunters. They struck at motion. I also knew that if I didn't move, it would most likely cease feeling threatened and skitter along on its way. I froze in place and waited.

I did not have these sorts of problems back in Wisconsin. We had Timber Rattlesnakes, but you literally had to go looking for them. They didn't just show up behind you while you were digging post holes like some sort of deadly-fanged ninja serpents. I don't even have a real fear of snakes! If you had a python, I'd touch it. I might even hold it. I don't dislike them, but the sudden prospect of getting two venom-filled hypodermic needles jacked into my calf made everything in my body start to tremble. The snake seemed to understand that something was wrong in its world. It seemed very disinclined to move along. I couldn't stay frozen forever. I started to get jittery. The post holer was still in my hands. I tossed it to my left. The movement and sound of it crashing distracted the snake. The second the little devil's head was turned, I bolted forward. I half-expected to feel the sting of a bite, but I didn't. I made it well out of strike range and kept running, a burst of adrenaline fueling my panic. It felt like I did a 200-yard dash in about two seconds flat. I flew into the middle of a field and proceeded to have a full-body, shuddering heebie-jeebies session.

In the midst of my freak out, I saw something that stopped me cold: the bay horse from the day before. I saw her standing on the far edge of the field, near the tree line. She was watching me again. On her rump were several long, ragged, bleeding gashes. Those were new. Something had attacked her, something large. A lion, perhaps, maybe a tiger? A cougar? Something had definitely tried to take her down last night. She saw me watching her. As if she knew that I was good for something like healing wounds, she started to limp toward me. She was clearly in distress. She was clearly hurting. I knew she needed help, and she knew I could give it to her.

I had no ropes, and I didn't want to rush back to the barn to get a rope in case she decided I wasn't worth her time. I waded through the grass toward her and met her halfway. Blood had run down her leg caking thickly in her short, fine coat. She had lost a considerable amount. The skin around the wounds was ragged and flapping. It looked like whatever had attacked her had done some serious muscle damage. I wouldn't be able to stitch it back together. It would have to be bandaged and allowed to heal. She would have problems walking for a while. She would be vulnerable in the wild, and she seemed to know it.

When she got to me, there was no hesitation, no concern on her part. She dropped her head and butted her broad face directly into my chest. I lifted my hands to her head and placed them on either side of her neck, up near her ears. The second I touched her, I felt her entire body relax as if she suddenly felt safe.

I'm not really a spiritual person. My parents weren't really religious, and my faith in any sort of higher power took a nosedive after the Flu, but at that moment, I felt like I was witnessing something larger than myself. I stood in that field holding that horse's head and something magical radiated between us. It was as if she understood that I would help her, and that she could trust me. It was a gift, an instant bond between us. It was powerful and brought a lump to my throat. I stroked her neck and told her everything was going to be okay. "C'mon, girl," I said. "Let's get you home." I turned and started walking back to the barn. After a moment, I heard the heavy footfalls in grass behind me, and I knew that she was following.

The bay walked back to the barn without balking. When I walked through the doors, she did not hesitate. She walked into the relatively cool interior of the barn and headed for the nearest stall without being directed.

The barn was a relatively newer horse barn. Five stalls stood on either side of the barn with a small tack room at one end. There was a small riding arena that I had repurposed into a night pasture for the cows. The large, sliding doors at either end could be opened during the day to let wind blow through. At night, the doors were closed and the cows were safe from predators. It wasn't an ideal multi-livestock facility, but for the moment, it more than exceeded our needs.

I closed the door to the bay's stall, and she almost dropped to the floor out of exhaustion. She was drained. It must have been an extremely eventful night for her. I walked to the large trough I had filled for the cows. I filled two large, rubber buckets with water and carried them to the stall, setting them in one corner. I gathered up a couple of pitchforks' worth of hay and tossed them through the stall window into a corner for her to munch. Then, I went to get supplies to treat her wounds.

Thing 1 and Thing 2 regarded me curiously from the pasture beyond the barn doors. "Say hello to your new sister," I told them. "No fighting. Mom and Dad love you all equally." The chickens, of course, did not seem to notice or care.

I ran to the house. I filled a pot with water from our filtering system, and then set it on the grate over the fire in the yard to heat. I got our first aid kit and a large bag of medical gauze Ren and I liberated from a hospital in Florida on our journey to Texas. The kit we assembled had been done under Ren's knowing gaze. As a trained nurse, she was the *de facto* doctor and surgeon between us. The first aid kit was stored in a massive toolbox that she had taken from a derelict hardware store solely for the purpose of being our "hospital" box. In it was everything we would need to perform minor surgeries and treat all wounds and illnesses. What it didn't have was medical supplies for animals. I had some stuff for treating worms and medical conditions for cows, but no horse things. I know that some people might think, "What's the difference? They're both big, lumbering beasts." I would have been one of those people two years ago. However, cows are ruminates, and horses are not. Cows have multiple, specialized stomachs. Horses only have one, like people. This makes them *entirely* different beasts on many levels. I would have to make a run to the nearest DVM office as soon as possible.

When the water was hot, I soaked a rag in it and then used the rag to clean the wounds in the bay's rump. She flinched and became a little distressed, but she did not shy away from me, kick, or bite. I took that as a good sign that she understood what I was doing to her needed to happen. Cleaning the wounds caused them to bleed afresh. Bright red blood seeped through the clotting and ran down her leg. The scars were ugly. In addition to the obvious, ragged tears, there were several smaller puncture wounds on her back and side. The creature that had attacked her had done a number on her. I wondered if it had been a single lion or tiger, or if a pair of them might have done the damage. Either way, she was clearly in bad shape.

Once I got the wounds cleaned, I used some hydrogen peroxide to clean them further, and then I slathered medicated salve into the cuts and punctures. I used large pads of gauze to cover the wounds and taped them in place with medical tape. There was not much else I could do after that, other than sit and wait for them to heal.

When my ministrations were complete, I saw the bay relax completely. Her eyes drooped. Her neck lowered. In seconds, she was asleep, able to fully rest in a safe place for the first time in who knows how long. I have never seen an animal in that stage of exhaustion.

I cleaned up the gear and left her to rest. Thing 1 and Thing 2, seeing that I had no treats for them, gave me the cold shoulder and returned to grazing in the paddock.

I washed my hands in what was left of the hot water and cast the rest of the pot into the garden. Any wastewater went to plants, always. I even urinated in the garden much of the time. I could not convince Ren to do that; she declined, citing the necessary apparatus to facilitate a directed stream. I couldn't blame her.

I went into the house to find something to snack on for lunch. Fester the Faithful Housecat was lounging in the kitchen window, watching the barn. He seemed to know someone new had arrived. I scratched him between his ears, and he immediately leaned into the attention, giving a low, throaty purr.

"This place starts to look more and more like a farm, doesn't it, buddy?" I rested in the kitchen, toweling off my sweaty face and head. I ate a pack of Zebra Cakes and drank a Coke. It wasn't a great lunch, but one of the few true benefits of surviving a world-ending virus was that all the Zebra Cakes on Earth now belonged to me, and there was no one to tell me not to eat them. Then, I went back out to continue digging post holes, making sure to monitor for snakes a little better. I could not wait until Ren came home from wherever she was that day so I could show her the new addition to the farm. It was probably the best wedding present I could have given her.

Ren returned in the early afternoon. She was lugging a bag of supplies. I happened to be facing the right direction to see her approaching, so I abandoned the post hole digger to give her a hand. "I don't know if I like you hauling heavy stuff—"

"—Stow it," she cut me off. "I am not a delicate flower. Women all over the world worked harder labor jobs than this well into their ninth month of pregnancy."

"Fair enough."

She squinted at me. "You look happy."

"Oh, I am," I said. "I got married to the most beautiful woman in the world today."

She started to smile, but turned it into a forced scowl. "Ease up, Romeo. Talk like that is why we *had* to get married." She patted her stomach.

"I got you a present today."

"Really? Was it Swiss Cake Rolls? Because I think I'm about to go into the house and eat every single box of those we have right now."

"Better." I couldn't hide my smile.

"Lies. There is nothing better than Swiss Cake Rolls."

"I think there is, but you can't eat it."

Ren rolled her eyes. "If I can't eat it, it's not that good of a present."

I led her into the barn and pointed at the far stall in the corner. "There."

Ren arched an eyebrow at me, but walked toward the stall cautiously. When she got close enough to see what was standing in it, she froze. Her jaw flopped open. She turned back to me with wide eyes and mouthed, *You got a horse?*

I nodded, practically bursting with pride. "Happy

66

Wedding Day, wife."

Ren put her hands on the side of her face in surprise. "This...this is amazing. Where? How?"

"She followed me home. Can I keep her?" I opened the stall door at stepped inside of it. The bay, somewhat more rested, moved toward me. I patted the side of her neck. "C'mon in and meet your new horse."

Ren was standing at the door of the stall. "I can't. I've never—"

"It's easy." I held out my hand for her. She took it and let me guide her into the stall. I moved her hand to the bay's neck. Ren looked like she was going to cry. I explained seeing her in the field after the hunt, and then how she came to me earlier that day. Ren's mouth hung agog at the story. She could not stop petting the horse. The bay did not seem to mind the attention.

"She is beautiful. What's her name?"

"That's up to you."

Ren thought for a moment. "I always wanted a horse. I bet every little girl goes through that horse-crazy phase. In my dreams, I had a boy horse called Ranger. That doesn't seem fitting for a girl horse, though."

"Girls could be Rangers, if they want to be."

"No...Ranger, in my mind, was an Appaloosa, and he and I would ride through Monument Valley in search of adventures. I don't think I could call a bay female Ranger. I would feel like I was betraying his memory." She thought for another long moment. "Hera. Hera was the goddess of marriage, childbirth, and family, and she came to us on this day out of all other possible days. Her name should be Hera."

It was a fine and fitting name for a horse, I thought. I stood and watched my new wife, pregnant with my future child, hug the neck of our brand new horse, and I felt wholly fulfilled. For the first time since the Flu left me alone on the planet, I felt like I was finally where I was supposed to be in the world, doing what I was supposed to be doing. I felt like I actually belonged in the world again, instead of existing as an aberration that should have died months ago. It was a wonderful sensation.

Ren and I had a lovely celebratory dinner that night. We ate the remainder of the javelina and smoked what we did not eat to preserve it. Ren made a soda bread and a simple pie with canned blueberry filling. We cracked open a bottle of sparkling apple cider, since Ren would not be drinking any alcohol for a while. We sat in our chairs by the fire and dreamed about the future. Everything was falling into place as it should. That night, for the first time in quite a while, I slept well.

Part Two
Fall

CHAPTER SIX

Horses, Cats, and Storms

The summer passed in the blink of an eye. It was so busy, I barely had any time to write in my journal. There was always something to that needed to be done, and never enough hours of daylight in which to do it. I built fences around pastures, I dug deep holes for a stockade wall, I was able to live-trap a couple of wild hybrid piglets *(they were something between a wild boar and a domestic white pig, and they started breeding quickly)* and brought them back to the farm, I got better at hunting and kept our protein needs fulfilled, and I worked with Hera.

In her first few days at the farm, I let the horse rest in her stall. I had to clean her wounds daily and change the bandages a couple times a day. After a few days, the scabs formed and it looked like I had successfully staved off infection. After a week, I noticed Hera was starting to get antsy from standing in her stall. I started letting her out into the riding arena at night to hang out with Thing 1 and Thing 2, and she seemed to like that. Every morning when I went to check on them, she would walk over to me let me pet her neck. It was very clear to me that she had been someone's pet before the Flu. Whatever domestication she had before everyone died was still lingering in her mind. Maybe she preferred the safety and consistency of domestic life to the freedom of roaming the plains? I could not speak for her, of course, but she seemed to enjoy being owned again.

After a week, I knew she needed to start exercising those wounded muscles. In the tack room of the stable, there were plenty of halters and lead ropes, so I would throw a halter on her head and take her for walks. At first, we started small, just around the perimeter of the farm. As her wounds started to look better, I extended those walks. I would take her down to the edge of the lake to inspect our water equipment. I would take her around the fields. I noticed that she was following me more like a dog than a horse. If I unclipped the lead rope from the halter, she was largely disinclined to wander away. She might stop to crop some grass here and there, but she would mosey after me before too long. It was like having a very large shadow. After a couple of weeks, I didn't even bother with the halter. I just opened the stall door, and she would follow. Ren thought I was crazy, at first. "She'll run away!" But, I felt like I knew Hera. I knew she would not run. And she never did.

It was that level of trust I had in her that convinced me to learn to ride. The closest I'd ever come to riding a horse in my lifetime was the time my family went to the circus and my dad let me ride one of the camels. I was by no means a natural horseman, but I knew that I wanted to be. It would be invaluable to have the ability to throw a saddle on a horse and be able to ride to hunting sites or take her out to scout the area. I could take Hera places I couldn't ride my bike. It only made sense. Horses would be the new/old four-by-fours of the post-societal wasteland. We were basically reverting to a pre-Industrial Revolution level of agrarian living, and riding a horse or having a horse pull a cart was going to be necessary once again.

I prepared for the first ride by reading about it, of course.

That is how I've had to do everything since everyone died. Books were my salvation and my instruction guides. I rode my bike to the library in nearby Atascocita and brought home every equestrian book they had on the shelves, as well a box full of magazines like *Western Horseman, Horse & Rider, Equus,* and *Practical Horseman.* At night, in the light of the fire in the yard, I read everything I could about riding, training, and horsemanship. I would explain what I read to Ren, even though she said she did not feel like she would be riding until after the baby was born. I also taught myself basic horse hoof care. I found rasps and clippers at a DVM office and brought them back to give her neglected feet a necessary trim. I did not trust myself to put nails through her feet, though. She would just be barefoot and carefree.

When I read enough to feel a little bit confident in what I was doing, I shooed Thing 1 and Thing 2 out of the riding arena and into the pasture. Then, I put Hera in cross-ties in the barn aisle. I brought out a bridle and saddle from the tack room. There was a lovely black leather Western saddle with a suede seat pad. With some polish and a little Murphy's Oil Soap, I repaired two years of neglect. I threw a saddle pad on her back, and swung the saddle up afterward. Hera craned her head around to look at what I was doing. I think she knew what was happening, or at least it was not unfamiliar to her. I fastened the cinch under her belly, adjusted the stirrups to the height I thought I would need, and straightened the saddle on her back. I eased her face into the halter, and she accepted the bit without fuss. After she was decked out, I led her into the riding arena. It was now or never.

Ren came to watch me. "I want to make sure you don't crack your skull open if you get thrown."

Her confidence in me was inspiring.

I positioned myself on Hera's left side. Holding the reins and the saddle horn in my left hand, and holding the cantle of the saddle in my right, I lifted my left foot into the stirrup.

Hera bore my fumbling with a saint's patience. After a couple of tentative bounces, I went for it. I stood in the left stirrup and went to throw my leg over the saddle.

Now, I had never, ever put a saddle on a horse before that day. Apparently, a cinch needs to be tighter than I had it. As I put weight in the stirrup and tried to straddle the horse, the saddle slid all the way to Hera's belly and sent me spilling into the dust of the arena. The sudden change in the saddle's position made Hera panic. She leapt away from me kicking out and trying to run. Luckily, she had horse sense. After a few seconds of running, she stopped and looked at me on the ground. The look on her face clearly said, *Not like that, genius.* From her seat on the fence, Ren howled with laughter.

Blushing from embarrassment, I reset the saddle on Hera's back and tightened the cinch properly. I tugged on the saddle a few times to make sure it was settled properly. When I was certain that it would not slide again, I tried again. This time, I was up and over, my right foot easily finding the other stirrup. I sat on her back and held my breath. Hera did not move. She gave a huff as if to say, *What now?* I tapped her sides with my heels and she lurched forward into a walk. And just like that, I was riding a horse.

Every day after that, I worked with Hera under saddle, both for her rehab and my own need to practice. It took me weeks to get to a spot in my training and development on horseback where I felt confident in what I was doing. Like I said, usually people did something, or they didn't do something. People who rode horses usually started young, and they usually had parents who taught them to ride, or they took lessons. For me to do this on my own, it was ridiculous. It was one thing to walk, and another thing entirely to trot, jog, and canter on horseback.

Hera did not have any problems accepting my commands, and whomever had trained her before I found her had done a splendid job. She responded to cues easily, and often seemed to know what I wanted her to do before I could tell her to do it. However, there was a large gap in my own trust in the horse where I had to learn that as long as I stayed centered over the animal, she would take care of me. When I coaxed her into a run, I had to trust that as long as I kept my balance, no matter how much it felt like I might fall off, she would make sure I didn't.

I counted myself extremely lucky that I was able to find a smart horse that needed help, and that had training before I came along. I did not have to go through the whole process of breaking her. That would have been a whole different mess.

One midsummer afternoon, everything came together. I was out on a ride with Hera, miles from the house, and I realized that I was no longer actively *thinking* about riding; I was simply riding. I was not scared. I had no need to grip the horn of the saddle. I just sat, coordinated my balance over her center of gravity, and let her take care of the rest. I had gone from analyzing everything I was doing, planning, and being conscious about it to simply *feeling* it. To be a good rider, there needed to be a fusion between man and beast, a simple connection between two creatures with both intent on the same goal. At that moment, with Hera doing an easy canter through the Texas fields, I became a horseman. There came with that realization a rushing sense of freedom, and a sense of purpose. I could not stop smiling.

The summer was not all horseback rides and happiness, though. A lot of our troubles came about because of the garden. First, I found out that gardening a large garden like ours was a daily occupation. It took time every day to walk through the plants and make sure they were all watered well. It took time to fend off the weeds which seemed to sprout overnight. It took time to fence off tender young plants from rabbits, mice, and bugs that would like to eat their succulent leaves and murder them before they had a chance to sprout fruits or vegetables. I spent a lot of time working in the gardens with Ren, erecting fences around them, and trying to refine our water system to keep up with the demand that plants needed during a hot, dry Texas summer.

I was using a three-bucket filtration method. I had a long hose running into the lake with a small electric water pump hooked into a quartet of solar panels for power to pump water to the buckets. It wasn't much, but it seemed to do the trick, for now. The three-bucket system was simple enough. It was made of three five-gallon buckets, each stacked on top of each other with a small hole in the bottom of the top two for water to filter down and through them, and a hole on the side at the bottom of the third for clean water to drain through a hose and a series of filtration screens into a holding reservoir. The top bucket held fine gravel, the second sand, and the third was activated charcoal. I had gotten literal *tons* of all that stuff hauled out to the farm before the RV died, maybe a decade's worth if not more. It was all stacked on pallets in garage of the house next door. To make the three-bucket system work well, it had to be filtering water constantly, hence the pump and the solar panels. As the farm grew, and our water demands grew, I had to keep adding buckets. Our single stack of three grew to a trio of stacks, and then to nine stacks. My simple three-bucket system had grown to a twenty-seven-bucket system. It was worth it, though. I piped hoses into the house and added hand pumps to the end of them so we could get water to places we needed it, like the kitchen sink and the bathroom sink. I was even working on figuring out a way to make a decent shower system so we could stop relying on a solar-powered camp shower for our bathing needs. Simply maintaining our water supply felt like it could have been a full-time job. We tried to practice conservation, as best we could. When you really had to labor for water, it became more precious. I missed the days I could take a hot shower for granted.

My long-term plans for our water system included figuring out a way to get the well pump in the basement of the house to start running again, and to start pumping up the well water from the aquifers deep below the house. We would have perfectly clean, clear water running through the pipes of the house again. It would almost be like returning to a pre-Flu existence. I salivated at the thought of that, yearned for it. However, for that to work, I was going to need a lot of electrical power. And all that electrical power was going to take a lot of work.

I spent many days of the spring and summer mounting solar panels on the roofs of the house, barn, and garage. It was a laborious, dangerous process that took many hours climbing up and down tall ladders, and hauling heavy panels to the roof with rope. I took an empty section of field and built a large framework to hold more solar panels. Using magazine articles, I learned how to wire the panels together and run long sections of electrical cords to an inverter that I had to wire into the main electrical grid of the house. It took a lot of solar panels (*less than I thought I would need, though*), but I actually managed to get enough juice running into the house so we could use electric lights at night. A few solar panels later, and we could run a TV and DVD player. The well pump and plumbing were on my lengthy to-do list. We were edging back toward civilization!

The night we got the TV working, Ren and I curled up on the couch in the living room and watched "Ghostbusters" and "Ladyhawke," both favorite movies of mine that Ren had never seen. Huddled under a lap blanket together, eating jelly beans, bathed in the blue-white glow from the TV screen, it was almost like being back before the Flu. It made us feel like we were just normal people again. More importantly, the solar panel kits allowed us to have simple luxuries like electric fans. The difference between sweltering to death on a still Texas summer night and being able to stick a box fan in a window to get some relief was everything, especially for a pregnant woman made miserable by the relentless heat.

That night we whispered our grand plans for the future. More solar power would get us a working hot water heater, and the electric well pump would pump clean, clear ground water into the house. No more bucket filters! No more running out of clean water. There would be a washer and dryer. There would be showers again. There would running taps. The more we dreamed, the more improvements we made, the more it seemed like it would all be possible. Maybe we were talking pie-in-the-sky, but it *felt* possible at that moment.

A hurricane hit the Gulf of Mexico late in the spring. Inland as far as we were, we were spared the brunt of the initial landfall, but the winds and rains were bad enough. Anytime there was rain, we tried to funnel as much of it into buckets for storage as possible. I had raided a few paint stores after we moved into the farm for just such a purpose. That was the only bright spot to it. We got a lot of clean, fresh water fast. The rain filled dozens of five-gallon buckets. The rest of the storm was terrible. It was several days of unrelenting rain and nasty winds. The wind ripped shingles and gutters from the roof and tore off three of the solar panels I'd mounted to the roof of the barn, doing damage to the underlying plywood in the process, damage that would need to be repaired. Wind-propelled debris cracked several more solar panels I'd mounted in the field near the house. All of them would have to be replaced. Winds and flooding killed a sickening number of plants in the garden, too. There was nothing to be done but replant and move forward. That was just how it was going to be. The extended growing season was also why I had moved south. There would be time to recover. If the plants could not recover, I would simply scavenge more. By this time, there were fruit and vegetable plants growing wild thanks to animals spreading seeds. It would be more difficult, but we would make it work. What other choice did we have?

The farm was not the only thing growing. Ren was a tiny-framed girl. It took almost no time for the baby to make its presence known. Her stomach began to bulge about two weeks after she revealed her pregnancy to me, and the burgeoning baby quickly asserted itself into her life. Her old jeans and shorts became too tight. She was able to find some maternity clothes at a nearby house, but the woman who had used them before was at least six or eight inches taller than Ren. Ren wasn't good with a sewing machine or needle, so she just used a scissors to lop off the excess leg and walked around with frayed hems.

The Texas summer heat made Ren cranky and uncomfortable. She was in a constant state of misery. She would sweat at the drop of a hat and had to make sure she was drinking a lot of water to keep from dehydrating. This, in turn, made her already baby-compromised bladder work overtime. "I swear to god, I'm either walking away from that toilet or going into it all day long. It's a miracle I get anything else done."

Even though there was a lot of fear in both of us associated with the pregnancy, there was also a lot of joy and hope. One night, in bed, I rolled over and curled my arm against her expanding belly, and as if claiming his space, a little foot lashed out and kicked my arm. I felt a tiny thump that startled me and woke Ren. She grabbed her stomach with one hand. "He's doing cartwheels, I think." We looked at each and other broke out laughing, equal parts nervous laughter and excitement.

I became very enamored with the baby. I wanted to see it. I wanted to hold it. I know that women have to do all the heavy lifting when it comes to carrying a baby, but I actually got envious of Ren's relationship with the little guy. I wanted to know what he was doing in there. She would occasionally groan and hold her stomach, or she would suddenly gasp and arch her back. I had no clue what was going on. I tried telling her that she was lucky because of that, and she offered to change places with me anytime, anyplace. The more she grew, and the more I thought about it, the more I really began to look forward to seeing the little bruiser.

We began to prepare for the baby in earnest, too. I rode my bike and cart to a furniture store and brought back all the baby supplies we would need in terms of a bed, crib, and changing table. I loaded them all into the house, and Ren set up a nursery. We started hoarding boxes of diapers. I rode to the one of the warehouse stores in Houston and brought back a cart full of disposable diapers for all stages of development from infant to toddler. With Ren riding in the cart, we went to nearby stores and took mountains of clothes, baby blankets, towels, toys, picture books, and everything else we thought we would need. The baby would want for nothing, we told each other. If it had the unlucky fortune being born into a world without other people, we were going to give it every advantage we could.

The first major problem we experienced came toward the end of summer. We had been on the farm for nearly a year. We had established a rhythm and flow to living there. We had adequately civilized the place, gaining electricity for the house and several animals to raise. I was on the verge of making the running well water dream a reality. I had holes dug for my stockade wall around the farm, but I could not figure out a way to plant the posts by myself. They were heavy and unwieldy. I could not get enough leverage under them to stand them up on end and plant them in the holes. It was just too great a strain. Ren, obviously, could not help. A skid loader would have let me make short work of mounting the posts, but that was not possible, either. I was stuck at an impasse. I needed a system of pulleys and ropes. I needed some tall stepladders, too. I could envision a way to do it in my head, but I simply did not have the necessary equipment. I would need to go into Houston to get the supplies. Because I did not want to take the long trip to get the supplies while there was too much to do around the farm, I postponed it. We had not had any issues for a year, we would be fine a few weeks or months more, I told myself. My mother used to say that if you tempt Fate too long, Fate will eventually give in to that temptation.

On a particularly hot, late summer night, Ren and I were trying to sleep. All the windows were open and we had a box fan running on full blast in the window and another large, oscillating fan at the foot of the bed. It was not helping. The fans only helped regulate our bedroom from "hellish" to simply "unbearable." We were both sweating and miserable. I had tried to be nice and massage Ren's sore lower back, but the heat of my touch made her recoil. It was so hot, a pregnant woman refused a back massage. If that's not hot, I don't know what is. I was staring at the ceiling and trying to remember what it was like to feel too cold. Outside, I started hearing our growing family of pigs squealing. It was heavy, panicked squeals. Fear. Terror. I knew why horror movies used to use the sound of screaming pigs as a special effect. It chilled the blood.

"What's that?" Ren sat up in bed. She pushed her bulging form off the bed and squinted through the screen at the barn. "I don't see anything."

I had already pulled on a pair of shorts and sneakers. I grabbed the shotgun I kept on a wall rack next to the bed and the MagLite I kept on the end table. I ran down the stairs and out to the yard. The sound of the pigs suddenly decreased a little. One of them was dead, I just knew it. I shined the MagLite toward the pens next to the barn. Reflected back was the tawny, golden coat of a massive African lion.

The thing was a large male with a thick, bristly mane surrounding a wide head, angular head. One of my younger pigs, already dead, was clutched in his massive jaws. His eyes lit up like fireworks in the glow from my flashlight. I felt prickles of energy along the scars on my back from where a tiger slashed me last fall. When you come face-to-face with a lion, your first instinct is to run. I was not allowed that luxury. I had a farm to defend. I had animals that needed me. I had a wife and child to protect. I had to run at it, shotgun raised. I dropped the MagLite with the beam pointing toward the pens. I needed two hands for the gun. The lion saw me coming. Contrary to every Tarzan book I've read, lions are not usually willing to attack a shirtless man. The lion had its dinner. It had taken easy prey. It turned and climbed over the fence of the pig pens carrying its meal, and disappeared into the night.

I took a few moments to survey the damage. The fence was still intact. The pigs had calmed down and stopped squealing. We still had several pigs left, so it was not as if this one being taken was going to break the farm, but I knew that a lion who knew where there were easy meals would be back. Maybe not the next night, maybe not the next week— but it would be back. I got angry. I ran after the lion and screamed curses at it. I fired at it, but I knew the shotgun wouldn't have the range to do more than give it a welt, at best. I fired the gun into the air a few times. I wanted it scared to come back. I knew it was a fruitless gesture, but I was powerless to do anything else.

The rest of the pigs were scared, but they were safe. I herded them into the riding arena to spend the rest of the night with the Thing sisters and Hera. I made sure the chickens were safely cooped. I checked and double-checked all the doors and closed the open windows on the lower floor of the house.

When I told Ren what happened, she looked worried. "Will it be back?"

It will. I knew it would be. I just didn't know when. "We are going to need to make the stockade wall a priority. The low fences aren't going to be enough to stop lions or other animals that decide to make our farm their personal buffet." I knew that building the wall would mean finally making that trip into Houston. I knew Ren didn't want me to go. She wasn't due for at least another month or two (without calendars, who knew for sure?), but she was getting *very* large and could not do everything she wanted to do around the farm anymore.

"How will you get there?"

I could take the bike, I told her, but I needed some heavy gear. I needed more power than I could generate personally. I would have to use the horse. I would have to make the bike cart a four-wheeled cart and figure out a way to hitch it to Hera. I could ride her, and she could get the cart home. "I'll need her pulling power."

"If you're loading a cart, it will be a lot to get there and back in a single day."

"Hera can do it. It will be a long, slow walk back, but we will make it work."

"It might take two days. Maybe three." Ren was not wrong.

"It might. Do you want me to stay?"

She nodded. Then, she shook her head. "No. No, this needs to get done. If we don't have the supplies to do it, we need the supplies. We need to protect the animals." Her hand moved to her belly. I knew what she meant.

"I will only be gone two days, at most. It won't be too bad. You can stay in the house with the doors locked and a gun on your lap, if you want."

Ren scowled at me. "I'm not a helpless delicate flower of a girl, schmuck. I will be fine."

"I know you will." I backpedaled. "It's just…I know how it can be when you're alone."

"I'm not alone. I'll have Fester."

It was settled, then. "I'll leave tomorrow as early as I can."

We slept, but only a little. I was out of bed by dawn. I rigged up a simple collar system to hook around Hera's neck.

I drove two pins through the ends of the bike cart arms and hooked the pins to the ends of the collar like a yoke harness, and then I added two simple wheels onto the front of the cart to make it so it could roll flat. It was an ugly cart, but once Hera was saddled and hooked to the harness, she could pull it with no real struggle. I threw a few pitchforks of hay into the cart and a five-gallon bucket of water, well-sealed with a lid. I grabbed my rucksack of tools and supplies, enough food for two days, and a blanket, just in case I needed it.

Ren came out to the driveway to see me off. "Keep a gun on you anytime you're outside, just in case," I told her. "I don't know if that lion will come back, but if he does, the sound of a gunshot will likely scare him off. If it doesn't, shoot to kill."

"I will." Ren looked grim, but I did not see fear in her eyes. This was just the way of things, now.

"And don't overexert yourself. Rest, if you feel like it. Sleep. I *can* stay home," I said. "I can do this another day, if you want. We can just keep the animals inside more."

"Don't be silly." Ren waved off my concerns. "Just come home to me as soon as you can, okay?"

We kissed. I stepped into the stirrups, threw myself onto Hera's back, and we set off. I glanced back over my shoulder to take a mental picture of my pregnant wife, standing in the driveway waving good-bye to me, with a fat, black-and-white cat doing figure eights around her legs. I waved good-bye to her, and she went back into the house. I didn't want to leave, but a stockade wall was a very necessary thing. I settled into the saddle for the long ride to Houston.

CHAPTER SEVEN

Alone on the Farm

Did I want him to leave? Of course not. When Twist first brought up the notion of him going into Houston for supplies so he could build the stockade wall, a large part of my brain thought about telling him no, but I did not want to be one of those women who freak out about every little thing. So what if I'm roughly the size of dwarf planet? So what if I have no idea how close I am to actually giving birth? So what if the thought of being alone in this house terrifies me right now? I was not going to break down and tell him that. I had made up my mind to live alone if I had to after my sister died. I had resigned myself to being someone who would have to struggle and scrape for everything she got in this new world, so I certainly was not going to go into codependent fits over someone who was actually trying to make our lives better. If he was strong enough to do all this work on his own, then I would be strong enough to let him go. He would return. *You will be fine. You will be fine. You will be fine.*

I watched him until the cart was out of sight. Then, there was nothing else to do but to keep on keeping on. There were still chores to do. There were still meals that needed to be made. There were still animals that needed looking after, and without Twist all that fell onto my shoulders. I went into the house and got my slim, black semi-automatic pistol. It was a slick-looking Sig Sauer. I practiced with it occasionally, and I think I was a better shot with a pistol than Twist. I liked carrying it, but I did not particularly enjoy the sound of it. It always felt a little profane to make a big noise in this quiet landscape. I could not fasten my gun-belt and holster around my waist any longer. The future Baby Stickler had expanded to enormous proportions, so I just slipped the belt over my shoulder like a purse.

Fester and I fed the remaining pigs. We fed the Thing sisters. We fed the chickens. I walked the perimeter of the property to check my live traps. I had caught two angry squirrels in the night. I was not about to start eating squirrel, so I let them go. I kept hoping for rabbits. In all the books I read, the quick-breeding of rabbits made them ideal for survivalists.

After I checked on the animals, I busied myself around the house. I swept and mopped the wood floors, and plugged in a vacuum to do the rugs. The solar panels were keeping us supplied with enough power to run a lot of our electrical items. How Twist figured out how to make solar power work is beyond me, but he spent several weeks reading books at night about electrical wiring and solar kits. He said that some people back before the Flu had such good solar power that they were able to kick energy back into their local grids, and then their power companies had to cut them checks for the surplus every month. I just looked forward to him getting enough power running through the house that we can have all the electrical power we need. A year ago, I was living by candlelight and scrap-wood fires in a Brooklyn flat. Now, I had a nice, big house in a beautiful part of Texas with electrical lights and a vacuum. It seemed so crazy to me. A year ago, I would have gladly cut off one of my toes to have a working TV again just to break up the boredom. Now, I have one. Granted, there is no more over-the-air television or cable, but at least we have a massive DVD collection. I don't take power for granted anymore. Every time I flip a light switch in the bedroom and the room is illuminated with clean, bright, white light, I say a silent prayer of thanks.

My "nesting" instinct started kicking in a couple of weeks ago. I read about that in one of the pregnancy books I picked up. It's apparently a common inclination of women heading toward childbirth. It is an overwhelming desire to clean things, get rid of detritus around the house, and prepare the home for the arrival of the child. My nesting was getting ridiculous. I wanted to sanitize everything. I had dozens of spray bottles of cleanser in my "store" home next door. I brought a couple of them over to the "living" house and started spraying down surfaces and scrubbing them a sponge. I heated water to boiling to kill any germs on the sponges first, and then I worked myself to near-exhaustion just preparing the house. It felt like nothing could be *too* clean. One of the pregnancy books I read said that the nesting instinct gets stronger when the baby gets closer to arriving. I hoped that wasn't true. I was not ready for this baby to arrive.

It wasn't that I didn't want him to arrive, of course, it's just that I was worrying about what kind of future he would have. I wanted everything to be perfect, and despite all our advancements in the past year, we were still a long way from perfect. The lion attack was certainly an exclamation point on that statement, but it was far more than that. I worried about our food levels, especially after we lost so much of the garden in the hurricane. Some of it had recovered to a degree, but was it enough? Could we have done more? I wanted to find canning supplies. I wanted a quarter-ton of mason jars and lids so I could make mountains of berry preserves and cucumber pickles and all that sort of long-lasting, easy-storing things that would sustain us if we hit lean times. I wanted to plant groves of fruit trees. I wanted to practice hunting. If Twist got hurt or incapacitated in some way, I knew I would have to pick up that slack. I wanted to get more animals. I wanted to get more fences around the house. I wanted that stockade wall. What if that lion had come during the day, and what if it had taken a precocious toddler instead of a pig? That thought, horrific was it was, played on a constant loop in my head. It felt like I would have to defend this child from the entirety of the world, and I was not mentally ready to do that. There was an old saying, *It takes a village to raise a child.* Well, what happens when there are no more villages, and everyone else is dead?

That first night in the house alone was the toughest. Twist and I had not been apart at night since the day we met. We slept in separate beds for a long time, but they were in the back of an RV and we were less than fifteen feet from each other. I could hear him snoring and felt the truck rock when he rolled over. When we finally broke down and began sharing a bed, I think it was more out of a need to know we were no longer alone than any sort of romantic desperation.

I hoped that Twist would be home by dark, but I knew in my heart that he wouldn't be. The ride to Houston was long. He needed to gather a bunch of supplies, and he didn't have any maps. It would be a long, difficult trek back. I don't care who you are—seventy or eighty miles on horseback in a single day was asking a lot. I had known he would have to camp somewhere. Luckily, camping was not all that difficult now. I did not figure he was on the plains huddled next to a campfire. He probably found a house, put Hera in the garage for the night, and slept on a couch or a bed. Knowing him, he would not have stayed in a house with corpses, so he might have had to search a bit, but there were plenty of houses out there. I did fear for his safety, though. How could I not? If something did happen to him, I would not know. If he died, I would only know because he would never come back. I might never know *how* or *where* he died. I would be left to agonize over that alone forever. That thought is what would keep me from sleeping.

The lower the sun got in the sky that day, the more apprehension welled up in my chest. I did not feel safe in the yard near the fire. I banked the coals for the night and retreated behind walls before it was even close to sunset. I secured all the animals in the barn to prevent the lion from getting another easy snack. I locked all the doors to the house and double-checked them to make sure they were really locked. I closed all the windows on the first floor. I brought a shotgun out from the gun safe and set it near the couch. I put my Sig on the end table next to the couch.

Fester curled up in my lap for attention, and I tried to watch a DVD to distract myself, but my heart and mind were not in it. I was too anxious to read. I suddenly felt old and very tired. The baby decided that he would try to cheer me up by doing a few dozen cartwheels. The little kicks on my stomach and bladder were annoying. It only soured my mood. I was too hot, too scared, and too uncomfortable.

I ended up wandering the upstairs hallway like some old sea captain's wife stalking the Widow's Walk. I kept looking out the windows that faced south, looking for any shadow that might be a horse and cart. I squinted out the window into the dark looking for a bobbing flashlight. I listened hard through the screen, trying to wade through the symphony of crickets, night bugs, and chirping frogs, for the sound of hooves on gravel or the squeak of the cart's wheels.

When I was fairly confident that it was after midnight and Twist had not returned, I tried to sleep. I lay in bed and rubbed my expansive belly with my fingertips. I tried to change my mindset and think of the positive experiences this child would have instead of dwelling so hard on the negative aspects. This baby would be the first child in generations to be raised completely free of the influence of television and mass media. Sure, he might watch a movie or a DVD of cartoons occasionally, but he would not be bombarded with advertising. He would not be subjected to nightly newscasts preaching doom and gloom. He would be free to learn to from books at his own speed. I would teach him math, science, and nursing. Twist could teach him…whatever he knows, I guess. Twist reads a lot; he can teach him literature and writing. The kid won't ever go to a "normal" school. He'll learn through books and experience, and he will be completely free of societal norms. No one will ever bully him. No one will ever make him feel *less than.*

Every time I start to build up that sort of rah-rah positivity in my head, my brain immediately chips in the negatives, too. This kid will never know romantic love. He'll never marry. He'll never have children of his own. He'll never have friends. He'll never play team sports. His whole life will be a struggle I've never known until I was in my twenties.

But, then I trumped that negativity by telling myself that I was still looking at this kid's future through my own eyes. I was used to being spoiled by modern society. I was used to cell phones, constant entertainment, and grocery stores. This world is a hardship on me because everything I used to have, I took for granted. This world is a hardship on me because I was not prepared for it, and I have had to play everything by ear since the moment I realized that I was not going to be dying by the wicked hands of the Flu. This child would only know the world he knew. He would have no memories of how easy we had it. He would accept everything as it was and adapt to it, the same way our ancestors did. They carved a life out of barren nature, and made it work for them. This child would not look at daily farm chores as a hindrance, but rather as something that we just did. He would see hunting as the only way to get fresh meat. He would know that farming was the only way to have a consistent source of vegetables and fruits. His world was going to be a wholly different experience than my world, and he would simply accept it as being the way it was.

I thought about telling the boy stories of "the good old days" when he was older. *We had stores with moving staircases! There were massive, tall buildings with boxes on cables that could take you from the first floor to the seventieth in only a few seconds! We used to have over three hundred channels of television, and the audacity to complain that there was nothing to watch!* It made me smile to think that my equivalent of the old "uphill both ways in the snow" adage would be things like, *Once, at a party, I ran out of battery power on my cell phone and couldn't take all the pictures I wanted!*

I thought about how hard my dad worked so my sister and I could have a decent life, and how much my mother struggled to make ends meet on my dad's meager income. We had a really nice life compared to some of our neighbors because both my parents worked so hard. My child would have a really nice life because hard work was the only way to live now. He would have everything he needed and nothing he didn't. The more I thought about that, the more it made me feel content. I was going to have a happy, healthy child. He was going to live, laugh, and work with us. He might struggle at times, but in the end, he would live and be alive. I knew in my heart that there were more people out there in the world. I knew there were was a colony in New York, and even though that colony was filled with psychos, I knew there had to be others out there in the world. Who could know what might happen in the future? Maybe the world would rebound somewhat. Maybe my boy would find a wife of his own someday and have a family. Maybe there would be actual villages once again, and his children, or his children's children would establish new governments, new sources of power, and new civilized cities. The blueprints were already established; it's not like they would have to be figuring out everything as they went along, they could just do it better. I just had to keep him alive, and keep trying. Anything was possible.

The world was illuminated by the light of a nearly full moon. It cast a pale glow across the landscape and I could see every inch of the bedroom in the gloom. For that, I was grateful. I did not want to wimp out and flip on my flashlight for any suspicious sound, nor did I want to plug in a night-light like a child scared of the dark. I was an adult. I was used to being alone at night. I was not going to break down and go into panic mode, but the fact that the moonlight was bright enough to read by made me feel immensely better.

In the distance, I could hear the yips of coyotes, and occasionally one of their thin, high-pitched howls would rise above the standard din of the late summer nights. I have not seen a coyote since I moved to Texas, but I had seen a couple of them in New York. I know they're mostly harmless, more scared of me than I am of them, but the sound of their howls in the dark never failed to raise the hairs on my arms and neck. There was something mournful about that noise. It was nothing compared to the long, low wails of wolves—I'd heard a couple of them in New York after the Flu—but it was still enough to make me go hyper-alert for a few moments afterward. Most of the time, when the coyotes called out, their calls would be answered with barks and howls from some of the dog packs that roamed the area. After the Flu, all the dogs that were freed by their owners, or were able to escape from their homes, merged into odd, mixed-breed packs for safety. Those packs quickly reverted to a semi-feral existence. I say semi-feral because sometimes, when I'm out scavenging homes, I'll see one of those packs. I know they're dangerous, but when they see me, there is always a faint look of recognition in their eyes, almost as if they are conflicted: do they keep roaming with their pack and enjoy freedom, or do they go back to the cushy life of regular meals and belly rubs? I would not mind having a dog around the farm. Especially now. I would love a pair of mastiffs or maybe a couple of Rhodesian Ridgebacks—something that would be willing to challenge or fight a lion. I know the expense would be high. Keeping a dog fed would require a lot of work. Most of the bagged dog food in the world has been destroyed by rats and raccoons. There were plenty of cans of dog food, and we would have meat scraps or maybe a full cut of meat for it, but still. Maybe someday Twist or I will come across a pup we can take home and domesticate.

I listened hard to the sounds of the dogs answering the coyotes. I could tell from the distance and direction that there were at least two packs of dogs within a mile of the farm. They weren't so close that I worried, but it was enough to keep me thinking. Twist insisted I carry a gun anytime I went scavenging. There were days I did not want to, but I always did. Hearing those dog packs was a good reminder of why I had to carry a weapon.

When I was in nursing school, I had to do an observation rotation at a hospital in my last semester of school. It was mostly hanging out and doing scut work, but occasionally interesting things happened. When I hit my rotation in the ER, I got to see a lot of gunshot wounds, or GSWs, as the doctors and paramedics called them. Seeing shot-up kid after shot-up kid, victims of gang violence all of them, made me hate guns. Now, I still hated guns, but the world was too dangerous not to have them. Running out of ammunition was always a concern in the back of my head.

A sudden howl rose up near the house. Very near. It made me pop out of bed like a ninja, pregnant though I am. My hand when to the gun on my bedside table, and I thumbed off the safety. It was a silly reaction. The animals were all safe inside. The windows and doors were locked. There was no way for the thing to get into the second story, but the nearness of the animal's howl scared me. It reminded me that there were things creeping around outside, and I had no way to track them at all times. They came and went when it pleased them, and I was not privy to their thoughts and movements.

Glancing out the window into the yard, I could see a

single, large dog. It looked wolfish, maybe a husky, maybe a malamute. It was just sniffing around the yard, looking for scraps. It probably smelled the remnants of the chicken we had slaughtered a few days ago.

I watched the dog curiously. Why wasn't it in a pack? It did not look scrawny or unhealthy. In fact, it looked strangely well-fed. It walked over to the pasture where the pigs were kept in the daytime. It sniffed around the corner where the lion had taken our pig. It marked the area twice with urine, and then disappeared into the shadows, never to be seen again.

The next morning, when I went out to inspect the animals and get them into their pens and paddocks for the day, I noticed fresh tracks around the pen, big, fat paw prints of a large cat. The lion had been back. Twist was right; any animal that knows of easy food would be back to exploit it. I would have to stay around the farm as long as the animals were out. I had planned on doing some scavenging, but I would have to go more than a mile from the house. That idea went out the window. I wondered if the husky had scared off the lion, or if the lion might have been tracking the husky.

I went back into the house and resumed my nesting cleanse. I found myself watching the paddocks far too often. If something was prowling around, the Things would probably react, and the pigs would start sounding alarms. My excessive watch was gratuitous and unnecessary, but I could not put the thought of a prowling lion out of my head. It made me very concerned for the baby in my belly. The Mama Bear in me wanted the lion dead. The nature lover in me wanted the lion to go away and never come back so I wouldn't have to shoot it. When I was a kid in Brooklyn, we only had to watch out for cars in the streets and the occasional gangbanger or crackhead. That seemed so much easier than dealing with rogue lions.

As the day progressed, I became more and more agitated. I would occasionally look out the south-facing windows, expecting to see Twist coming down the road with a loaded wagon, but the road stayed empty. By the time midday rolled around, I forced myself to eat some lunch, but I was not hungry. Even my beloved Swiss Cake Rolls tasted like sawdust. I tried not to think of worst-case scenarios, but my hormone-addled brain could not help but leap to wild, horrible conclusions. *He's dead*, said my brain. *You're alone.* I had to remind myself that Twist was a strong, capable young man. He'd been alone in the wilds of the world long before he met me, and he faced them without fear.

But, here's the thing: He *should* have been back by midday, at the very least. If he got to Houston yesterday morning and spent all afternoon securing his supplies, and even if he camped in Houston all night, if he started back on the road this morning, he should have arrived home. I started getting worried and angry. Fester noticed my mood and tried to cheer me up by rubbing his head on my shins in an attempt to curry attention from me, but I had no time for him. Something was wrong. I could feel it.

I spent the afternoon pacing the house. The sky was dark with clouds. The longer the day went on, the darker the clouds became. A storm was coming. Judging from the way the sky looked, it was going to be a bad storm and Twist and Hera would be stuck in it, somewhere. The longer the day wore on, the more my level of worry increase. The baby knew something was up. He got active. *Really* active. It was like my worrying was making him worry. I felt a wrenching pain low in my abdomen, like lightning across my pelvic bone. It was so great, it dropped me to my knees and made it hard to breathe. Message received, baby. Message received. I retreated to our bed, despite it still being very light out. I propped up pillows behind my back and tried to reduce my stress through meditative breathing. *Twist was fine*, I told myself. *You will be fine. You will be fine. You will be fine.* I recited my mantra on a loop in my brain. Deep breath in, hold it, deep breath out.

The afterimage of that blast of pain lingered, though. I could not concentrate it away. It felt too low to be a contraction, but I wasn't sure. This baby arriving early would be part of a worst-case scenario. Prior to the development of NICUs, premature birth mortality was over 95 percent. I wasn't sure this baby had cooked long enough. He might have. It was so hard to keep track of the days, especially in Texas where the spring, summer, and fall all looked pretty damn similar to this northern girl who was used to snow melting, April rain, July heat, and the leaves changing in September to signify seasonal transitions. As a nurse and someone who knew something about emergency medicine, my mind involuntarily went through the Rolodex of symptoms and potential disasters that could befall a pregnant woman.

Stop it! I had to scream at my brain. Panic and worry would not help. I went back to meditation, but I could not clear my thoughts. I wanted Twist to be home. I wanted the stockade walls built. I wanted the lion dead. I wanted the feral dogs to go away. I wanted everything at once, and it began to overwhelm me. My pulse elevated. My mind raced. The apocalypse was no place for a baby. Why did I think I could do this?

As if to punctuate that thought, a clap of thunder snapped out of the sky, harsh and crisp. It sounded like lightning hit the window, it was so loud. I felt my stomach twinge again. The darkening sky, after threatening all day, became intense and violent. I looked out at the sky to the west and saw a massive wall of black clouds rolling toward the house. Lightning was spitting from the front, and a curtain of heavy black rain fell beneath the leading edge. The storm was going to be bad. Very bad.

CHAPTER EIGHT

Houston

The Flu was something of an enigma to me. By the time the newspapers and cable news channels realized it was a problem, there was only about a week of actual reporting on the situation before the electrical grids went dark and all communication was blacked out. Most people were dead or dying by that point. The last image on TV was the President telling everyone that we were pretty much doomed, but if anyone survived we should continue on in the best traditions of America.

The last week of television was filled with a lot of pundits trying to find a scapegoat for the Flu. The Big Three networks gave up on programming and went to twenty four-hour news coverage until all their on-air talent was too sick to continue. I remember the talking heads on TV casting a lot of blame. One channel blamed the Russians. One channel said it was a viral weapon attack from some Mideast extremist group. Another channel said it was the fault of our own government, a lab experiment gone bad. The right-wing channels blamed liberals. The left-wing channels blamed conservatives. They all spat venom and vitriol at each other, everything, and everyone until there was nothing left but silence. The final week of television was spent with people desperately trying to find answers and cast blame. It was sickening. In the end, the left-wing and right-wing, the religious and the atheists, the rich and the poor—they all ended up dead and decaying. The Flu was the Great Equalizer.

Until the Internet stopped working, I spent a lot of time desperately seeking answers. What caused the Flu? Where did it start? Was there anything that was showing promise as a cure? All I knew for certain was that the airline hub cities went down first, and then the virus spread out to the small communities from there. Houston was a hub city. Houston got hit hard. George Bush International and William P. Hobby Airport were ground zero for the virus in Houston. Anyone taking off or landing from Houston became a carrier of the virus within the first week. Same with all airports, but given the size of the two airports in Houston, the virus was spread very quickly throughout the area, and then onto the rest of Texas.

A person gets on a flight in a city. He lands in Houston—boom! Infected. He won't know he's infected for at least thirty days. That was the length of time it took for the virus to fully infect its host to the point of showing symptoms. However, during those thirty days, the virus was reproducing and shedding at an alarming rate. Simply passing by someone with the virus was enough to get you infected with it. For thirty days, that person with the virus infected every single person they came into contact with in his daily life. At work. At the grocery store. At church. At the mall. At sporting events. At schools. On public transportation. Those people that got infected by that one person all went about their daily lives, shedding virus to those that they knew. Within five weeks, they would be dead, and they didn't even know it. The virus took a little more time to filter out to the smaller towns and communities, but it got there. No one was safe. It was impossible to be safe. The Center for Disease Control declared it a world-killer the day before TVs went dark. Only those of us lucky enough (*or unlucky enough, maybe)* to be born with a natural immunity to the virus would survive.

Because of Houston's status as a hub city, it got hit hard and fast. The panic set in quickly as soon as people started dying in great numbers, and thus, the city went into full riot mode. Stores were looted. Buildings were burned. Gun battles broke out in the streets over supplies like canned food and water. It was chaos. For a week. And, then everyone went to the Great Sleep, and peace reigned in the city once again. That week of chaos messed up the city badly, though.

It took me most of the morning to just get to what I considered to be the edge of the city proper, and the better part of another hour of riding to get to where the major stores were located. Houston, like most major cities, was a tight city center surrounded by sprawling suburbs of various levels of wealth. The first time I went into the city after we settled on the farm, I had been shocked by the destruction of the city. It was bad. Clearly, a year of no humans had not done the city any favors. There was evidence of severe damage, maybe a hurricane, maybe a tornado or two. Dozens of buildings were ripped apart in swathes. Debris was scattered in fields around them. The stores had been well looted during the final days of the Flu. Some stores had been looted in Madison, sure. But, not to this level and extent. Entire stores had all the goods ripped from the shelves and piled haphazardly in the aisles. People had started fires in the middle of stores just to start fires. Liquor stores were empty of everything but dust. One thing that never failed to make me laugh was the fact that people thought to steal all the lottery scratchers at convenience stores. What was the thought process behind that? *Man, if the world doesn't die, I'm totally going to be rich!*

I had a basic road map for Houston, one taken from an atlas. It showed me the streets and highways, but it did not have locations for things like Home Depot or Lowe's. Those I had to guess at. The branded store signs high atop tall metal spires helped me locate them, but I still had to get close enough to see them on the horizon.

I learned early on in my post-Flu survival that I should always take more than I thought I would need. I spent the entire afternoon going to various stores and loading up on the things I would need to erect the stockade wall. I got tall stepladders, scaffolding platforms and pipes, pulleys, ropes, hand-crank winches—you name it, I was throwing it in the cart because who knows what I might need.

Hera suffered through the afternoon in silence. I brought her inside the buildings to get her out of the sun and let her cool down, but she still had to stand next to the door because I couldn't get the cart through most of the doors. I had to make sure to get her water to keep her hydrated. I gave her a pile of grass to munch on to keep her occupied. At the same time, I could not stray too far from her. The feral dog packs in Houston were large. A horse tethered to a heavy cart would be easy prey for them.

It had taken me all of an hour to know that I would not be getting back to the farm the same day I left. The supplies were everywhere. I had to wade through a disaster scene and pluck out the useful bits. It was not like I could just walk in and pluck what I needed from organized shelves. Everything I found took work to get, and more work to load into the cart. I resigned myself to having to camp overnight and getting back to the farm the next day. When I made that decision, the next step was to make sure I came back with as full a cart as Hera could manage. If I was going to make a two-day journey to Houston, I should come back fully loaded.

I waded through clothing stores, housewares stores, and hardware stores. Anything that might be valuable or useful went into the cart. I found stockpiles of diapers and mason jars. I added more solar panels to replace the ones that were destroyed in the storms. I got spools of electrical wires and specialized tools to add more power to the house. I got electric saws and cordless drills with large battery packs. Having electrical power again was a treat. Things that I thought I would never be able to use again were once again valuable and useful. I got a food processor for making baby food. We would need that, eventually.

I went to one of the hospitals on Houston's north side and took as many supplies as I could hold. I was able to open the double-doors to the lobby and walked Hera into the cool darkness of the lobby, shutting the doors behind her. Hera's nose wrinkled at the lingering stench of death. All the hospitals were mausoleums now. Even in the lobby, I could see bodies scattered about like cordwood. Desiccated corpses slumped on the waiting room chairs, on the floors, and on gurneys. I had to tiptoe over bodies to get to the supply closets. In the final days of the Flu, the nurses and doctors, all battling their own symptoms, had waged a valiant war against the virus, but ultimately, all of them died in their scrubs, slumped on desks or curled up on the floors. As bad as I felt for the patients who died scared and miserable in beds or in waiting rooms, I felt worse for the medical professionals who gave their all in a hopeless, losing effort. They were the real heroes of the last week of the Flu.

Leaving one of the hardware stores, Hera began to get antsy. I saw her eyes roll to the side. Following her gaze, I saw what had her on alert: a grizzly bear, a massive mound of muscle and thick, coarse brown fur, had just ambled around the corner of the building. Grizzlies were, of course, not native to the Houston area. Likely, he had been in the zoo. It did not make him less dangerous, though. The beast stopped not more than thirty yards from us. He looked as shocked to see us as we did him. I carefully moved toward the shotgun I had in the cart. I had no idea if a shotgun would be enough to kill a grizzly bear, but if I must, I would try. The bear surveyed us for a few moments. He was thick and round. He must be eating well. I tried not to think about what he was eating to keep himself so healthy. After several tense moments, the bear decided that we were not worth investigating further and continued on his easy, unhurried pace through the cityscape.

As the sun dropped lower in the sky, I knew I needed to find some sort of shelter for the night, someplace where I could get Hera fenced in and safe, and then get the saddle and harness off her. She needed a break from being the proverbial workhorse. I wander through the side streets of the northeast side suburbs. Eventually, I found house with a three-car garage that was empty of corpses. I don't know why I have such a problem with sleeping in a house where someone died, other than to say that I just do. It bothers me. I hate feeling like I'm disrespectful to the dead. I feel guilty, too. I feel like I should give them a properly burial or funeral. If I did that for every body I found, I would never stop digging graves, though. Life is for the living. I could not help the dead.

I had to use tools to defeat the locks of the house, and in doing so I rendered the front door lock useless. I set the cart down in the driveway of the home, freeing Hera from the harness and saddle. Then, I fed and watered her. The five-gallon buckets of water I hauled from the farm were warm, but it was clean water. I could not do better than that. Hera drank deeply. She seemed to be glad to be free of the saddle. I put her on a picket line in the front yard to graze. I don't think I had to picket her; I think she would have stayed near me, regardless, but it gave me peace of mind.

Then, I built up a small fire in an adobe brazier that I found on the porch of one of the neighboring houses. I used scrap twigs and old newspaper for kindling, and I found a chunk of wood on someone's porch for the main fuel. I heated a can of beef ravioli for dinner and ate it with a plastic spoon. Then, there was not much else to do than go to sleep. I put Hera in the garage, feeling guilty for making her stand on hard concrete all night. She did not seem to mind. The moment the doors of the garage closed, she gave a sigh of relief and drowsed. I left the interior garage door to the house open so I could hear her if she began to panic, and I collapsed on a dusty couch in the house's living room.

I slept too easily that night, utterly exhausted from the long ride and subsequent scavenging. I was too complacent, I think. Maybe I was getting to the point where I was just used to being alone in the world. My grandparents lived in a small town in Colorado. They never locked their doors. They did not fear attack or burglary. They just thought they were safe because they knew everyone in town, and most of their neighbors did the same. I used to think that was insane. I locked doors whenever I could. In the library in Wisconsin, I built barricades for the doors. On the farm, I locked the doors every night. When I was somewhere I could not lock doors, I would turn into the world's lightest sleeper. The confused sigh of a mouse having an existential crisis would have woken me. That night, though—I don't know. Chalk it up to being too used to being alone, I guess. I slept, and slept hard.

I suppose that's why waking up to a shotgun in my face shook me so hard.

A pair of men, neither physically imposing, were in the living room of the house. They were dressed simply in jeans and worn flannels over dirty white tees. One had a Houston Astros ball cap. The other was had long, dirty hair. The one with the shotgun said something in Spanish when he knew I was awake. *"Levanta les manos!"*

I do not speak Spanish. I had a basic introduction to it when I was in junior high, but I did not pay a lot of attention. Luckily, I was able to interpret based on context and my knowledge of Mystery Science Theater 3000. I knew "manos" meant hands, as in the classic MST3K episode where they watched "Manos: Hands of Fate"—easily one of the top five worst movies of all-time. When someone jabs a gun in your face and says something about hands, usually they want you to raise your hands and don't move. I assume "levanta" means something akin to "put up" or "raise." I slowly raised my hands, too shocked and stunned to see other living people to do anything but comply. Besides, I was flat on my back on a couch. I was not about to Jason Bourne the situation; I'm not that kind of guy.

The guy with the shotgun gestured with the barrel for me to sit up. I did, keeping my hands straight up in the air. The other guy was rooting through my ruck of supplies. He pocketed my ammunition and took my shotgun for himself. The two armed men gestured for me to walk to the door of the house. I started to, but I stopped. What was the Spanish word for horse? *Vaquero?* No, that was…cowboy? Cab-something, wasn't it? I moved toward the door cursing myself for not taking Spanish class more seriously. *Caballo?* That sounded right. How could I make a sentence?

"*Caballo!*" I said. I pointed toward the garage. How do I say "release my horse?" *Libre?* "*Libre mis caballo, por favor!*"

The two men froze. The one holding me in his sights said, "*Habla Espanol?*"

I shook my head. I could not say I spoke Spanish, in all honestly. "*Habla Engles?*" I asked.

The two men looked at each other. One shook his head. The one who took my gun went to the garage. He said something to his friend. I recognized the word for horse. He went to the garage doors and opened one, giving Hera free access to the world. He shooed her outside. She did not run, but rather regarded him curiously.

The one with the gun on me said something that I interpreted as "get walking." I walked out the front door, stomach tight and head spinning. Strangely enough, I was not scared. I did not feel like these two were going to shoot me. I mean, they certainly could have. They had me dead-to-rights. I never would have even known it. There would have been a flash of sound and then nothingness. I would not even have known I was I dead. The two Latino men were jittery and worried-looking. I think they were as scared of the future as I was, and they were worried about their things being stolen. Maybe they were alone in this world, too. I know how I felt when I found someone else besides me. It was a shock. Granted, it was a joyful shock to me, but a shock nonetheless.

I let them walk me out of the house and into the street. Hera still stood in the yard. She looked confused, too. The men took up points on either side of me. One led the way down the street in the dark, the other followed me, shotgun trained on the small of my back. He stayed back several steps to make sure I couldn't spin around and ninja the gun away from him. *(Not that I could have, anyway.)*

We walked several blocks in silence. The moonlight illuminated the suburban street well enough that we could see every detail, all the overgrown lawns, all the dead, abandoned cars along the sides of the road and in the driveways, all the damage to the siding of the houses. We stopped in front of a large, three-story McMansion. I could see the faint glow of lights inside. Someone else was in there.

The men led me to the front door, and they knocked on it. After a moment, the door opened and a teenage girl was standing there. She saw me and her jaw dropped open in shock. It took her a second to recover, and then she said something in Spanish. One of the men replied. I felt the barrel of the gun poke me in the small of the back. I moved forward, following the first man. They led me to a small bedroom and shoved me into it. The door closed. There was no exterior lock on the bedroom, but I knew they were armed and probably did not want me deciding to leave.

I sat on the bed in the corner of the room and waited. I was nervous. What was going on? Who were these men and what did they want? And, of course, my thoughts drifted to Ren and the baby. I needed to get back to them. I needed to see her again. I needed to hold that baby. I can't explain it, but I felt a change in my fundamental make-up right then. Maybe it was a reorganization of my perspectives. At that moment, I knew what I needed to do. It only took me a split second to decide, but I knew that whatever I had to do to get back to Ren, I would do. Even if that meant having to kill someone.

I am not a killer. It took me two years to actually hunt an animal for food in this post-apocalyptic world. I still have nightmares about the day I had to kill a cow because it was suffering. However, I also knew that I had someone who depended on me as much as I depended on her. I knew that there were no rules in this new world. Kidnapping was not a crime any longer. Those who held the guns made the rules, and the rules were always changing. I would play nice as long as I had to until I saw an opening, and then I would either make a break or kill anyone who stood in my way. I did not want to kill someone, but I would do what must be done. I just hoped it would not come to that.

I waited in silence. A single candle burned on a wax-covered candle holder on an end table next to the twin-size bed. The bed was dirty. The sheets needed to be washed. I looked out the window of the bedroom. I could see a fire burning in the backyard. At least three people were gathered around it, and though the screen I could hear the muffled sound of conversational Spanish. It was far too fast for me to know what they were talking about, but I didn't think they were discussing baseball. I heard the word "gringo" once. That had to be me.

Eventually, the door to the room opened. A woman came in with a paper plate of food and a can of pineapple Fanta. She smiled at me, and held out the plate. It looked like an enchilada. I took it from her. "Gracias." The woman smiled and nodded at me, and then backed out of the room. Not knowing what else to do, I ate the enchilada. It was delicious. I could have happily eaten a dozen more.

The next time the door opened, the man with the shotgun

was there. He wasn't pointing the gun at me, though. He motioned for me to exit the room. He led me downstairs and into the backyard. Gathered around the fire were five people: the two men who found me, the teenage girl, the older woman, and an older man with a salt-and-pepper beard. All were Latino, but they did not look related. They all had varying skin color shades and facial features. They were dressed in shabby clothes, but they looked well-fed, like they were surviving all right.

The older man said something to me in Spanish, and I shook my head. "*No habla.*"

The teenage girl piped up. "He asked your name." Her English was heavily accented, but quite good otherwise.

"Oh, I'm Twist. What's your name?"

She translated. The old man nodded. He pointed at himself. "Enrique." Then, he pointed around the circle. "Paco. Guillermo. Maria. Luciana."

"Call me Lucy," the girl said. The old man spoke again. "He wants to know what you were doing in our neighborhood. He wants to know if you were trying to steal our things, take our food."

"Me? Stealing?" I shook my head. "No. Not at all. I didn't know anyone lived in this neighborhood."

Enrique said something else. Lucy translated. "He says, then why were you here?"

These people seemed like decent folks. Their situation was my situation. We were all just trying to make a go of it in a world where civilized rules no longer mattered. For all they knew, I was armed and could have killed them in their sleep. However, as much as I wanted them to know the truth, with the possibility of forming alliances and perhaps friendships, I did not know them well enough to take that leap of faith at the moment, not with a wife and baby to protect. I tried to walk the fine line between the truth and a lie. "I was just bedding down for the night before getting back on the road. I meant no harm. I did not know anyone else was alive."

Enrique said something else. Lucy said, "He wants to know where you live."

"Nowhere, really. I move around a lot, looking for other survivors." That wasn't quite a lie. I had done that for a while.

Guillermo, the one holding the shotgun, said something. Enrique nodded. Lucy said, "Then why did you have a cart full of building supplies?"

"I was trying to find a place to settle down." It was as good a lie as I could come up with at that moment.

Lucy translated and Enrique nodded. He spoke again. Lucy asked me, "Where did you get the horse?"

"Family pet from before the Flu."

Enrique nodded as Lucy translated. He seemed to buy that answer. He spoke again. Lucy translated. "Why didn't you stay on your farm to settle down? Why are you roaming?"

"Not enough supplies on the farm."

Enrique seemed to accept this answer. He sat down in a lawn chair and gestured for me to sit, as well. He said something to Paco. Paco went into the house and came back with cans of beer. He handed them around to everyone, even Lucy. By my estimates, Lucy looked to be fifteen or sixteen. I reminded myself that there was no drinking age anymore. I accepted the offered beer. It was warm, but I did not want to offend.

Enrique spoke again. Lucy said, "We are not bad people. Enrique worries that you have friends nearby. He worries that you are coming to kill us or enslave us. He has seen other white people in Houston doing that."

"There are other people?" It blurted out of me before I could stop myself. "I haven't seen anyone in months."

Lucy nodded. "There are a fair amount of people ranging around Houston. Paco and Geemo have seen them."

Guillermo said something. Paco agreed. Lucy translated. "There are at least three main groups of survivors in Houston. One group is made up of mostly white people. One group is mostly black people. The third group is mostly Latino. There may be more."

"Why are you separated from the groups, then?"

Lucy shrugged. "It is dangerous in the city. Those three groups are fighting each other for supplies and territory. We don't want any part of that."

"I don't, either." I felt a little dispirited at the news that there was something of a race war still going on inside the city of Houston. I had thought that if there was something that could make us forget the stupidity of lines of division that it would be a massive tragedy like the Flu.

Enrique rattled off a long monologue. Lucy tried to translate as he spoke. "He says that he doesn't want to let you go because he thinks you're holding back information. You could be in league with one of the three groups in Houston. He doesn't want you reporting back to them. You could bring bad things onto us, and we have been working very hard to stay out of their sights."

"I don't want to harm any of you. Honestly." I hoped I sounded sincere enough, because I certainly meant it.

The five people spoke amongst themselves in rapid-fire Spanish. I couldn't follow any of it. I would snag a word here and there, just basic vocabulary, really. I had no idea what they were debating. It was clear that Maria and Lucy were in one mind, and Paco and Guillermo were of another. Enrique listened to them all. When they were done debating, Enrique turned to me and spoke. Lucy waited until he was done, and then she translated. "He says that he wishes he could trust you, but we have worked really hard to build a life for ourselves here. If you are part of one of those groups in the city, you could bring your people back here and destroy everything we have built."

"But, I'm not. I'm from Wisconsin."

When I said Wisconsin, Paco's face lit up. "Go Packers!"

"Packer fan?" I asked.

He nodded. "Aaron Rodgers. *El major*."

108

Paco was clearly a man of great taste and sophistication. "He was certainly the mayor of Titletown."

Enrique said something harsh, and Paco stopped smiling. Enrique said something to Lucy. She, in turn, said to me, "Enrique says he wants to trust you, but he can't right now. He wants you to stay with us for a day or two so we can survey our perimeter and make sure you don't have anyone looking for you."

I did not want to stay with them. They seemed like nice people, but I had to get back to the farm. If I wasn't back by noon, I could see Ren going out of her mind with worry. I did not want to tell them that I had a pregnant wife, though. I did not want them to know that I was a day's travel from them, with a farm, supplies, and fresh water. Until I knew them better, that was a dangerous tightrope to walk. It could go badly. I started playing different scenarios in my head. Part of me wanted to bolt. Part of me wondered if I could leap out of the chair and snatch the gun from Guillermo before he gunned me down. Maybe I would play along with them and just try to sneak out during the night. I did not like feeling like a prisoner, but I didn't see any other choices for the time being. "I really don't want to impose on you, I said. You have your own thing going, and I would just like to get my horse and be on my way."

Lucy translated and waited for Enrique's response. Lucy's face fell as he gave it. She told me, "He says that he has to protect us. He asks that you be patient and understand, because he is certain that if your roles were reversed, you would want to do your homework, too."

And like that, I was a prisoner of my new friends. They let me attend to my bodily needs, and then Guillermo walked me back to that bedroom. When the door closed, I heard them fiddling around outside with the handle. After a few minutes, I tried the door and found it wedged shut, probably with a chair. My heart sank. I was on the second-story of a nice house. The window of the room had a screen in it, but it was only about fifteen feet to the ground outside. I could jump it, easily. I would probably not break a leg or turn an ankle if I tucked and rolled. I saw Paco start walking a guard route around the tall fence in the backyard, shotgun on his shoulder. They were going to stand a watch all night. I wondered if they did that regularly, or if this was something special because I was there. Either way, I was trapped. Granted, it was an almost pleasant sort of trapped. They seemed like decent people who just wanted to protect themselves from an unsavory element. I understood that. Ren knew I might camp, so I still had time to get away in the morning. I would figure things out later.

I flopped down on the bed and tried to relax. My chest felt tight, my stomach hurt, and I was worried. I had to tell myself that everything would work out for the best. My mom used to say that most people were good people. I felt like these people were good people. They fed me. They didn't kill me when they had the chance. They were rational. Everything would work out in the light of day.

Sounds at the door woke me. I sat up in bed and glanced out the window. It was just after dawn. A front had moved in sometime during the night. The clouds were dark and gray, oppressively low in the sky, and the winds had kicked up a fair amount. The trees I could see from my window were being moved considerably by the winds.

When the door opened, Lucy was there with a plate of fried eggs and some sausage. "It's not much. We have a few pigs and chickens. That's about it."

"It's great. Thank you." I took the plate from her.

She stood in the doorway and watched me eat it. "Enrique went down the road and inspected your cart. He says you weren't gathering survival supplies. He says you were gathering housing supplies."

He had me there. I lied to her. "I was gathering things so I could settle down and stop roaming. The future is going to be in farming. I was going to find a decent place and fix it up. Plant some crops."

Lucy glanced down the hallway. She translated what I said into Spanish. After a moment, Enrique's face peeked around the frame of the door. He spoke. Lucy said, "He says you already have a place. The cart is not stuff you would normally get when first starting out. He also says you have a baby, because of the diapers."

"Just preparing for any emergency, I said."

Enrique's face flared at the translation, and he spat out something harsh in Spanish. I didn't need Lucy's translation to know he'd just called me a liar.

I decided to change my angle and asked him to sit down. Through Lucy, I spent twenty minutes telling Enrique my story. I told him about Wisconsin, about burying my parents and girlfriend, about surviving the winter and bringing the RV south to find a new life. I left out Ren. I felt a need to protect her from this, if I could, which I don't understand. Ren was half-Venezuelan. I think she spoke Spanish. I probably should have told them about her.

When I had Enrique buying into my story, I changed just enough of my tale to throw him off, should he and his people come looking for us. I told him that I found a small commune of ten people about forty or fifty miles northwest of Houston. I figured fifty miles was a daunting enough slog to prevent them from casually wandering out that direction, but it was believable that a man on horseback could ride that distance in less than a day.

Enrique watched my face carefully and listened to my words. Eventually, he nodded, scratching at his chin. He shrugged and talked to Lucy. They exchanged a few sentences each. Finally Lucy said, "Enrique says he believes you. He wishes you had just told him the truth to start, though."

"We all have to do what we can to protect our people, don't we?"

Lucy translated. Enrique said something in return. Lucy said, "He says maybe there will come a day, hopefully soon, where we won't have to lie to each other, and we can all be brothers again."

Was he going to let me go? I smiled. "I'd like that." I stuck out my hand. Enrique smiled and shook it.

Lucy translated his words. "He says he's sorry we had to do this."

"Me too, but I understand."

"He says he would like to come see your commune someday."

"I would like that, too."

"He also says that he would like it if you took care not to be seen leaving this neighborhood. We have gone to great lengths to hide ourselves outside the interior city. So far, no one has noticed us until you stumbled in here."

"I will do my best." I stood, and Enrique led me to the door of the house. He returned my shotgun unloaded, but handed me some shells. I accepted the weapon and walked out to the road. They shut the door front door, but I knew they were watching.

As soon as I could, I started jogging down the road, heading back toward the house where I had to leave Hera and my cart. The cart was still there, but the horse was not. My heart fell. I gave a couple of low whistles and called for her. I ran around the houses in the neighborhood looking for her. No dice. I found a pile of her special blend in the street, but it was hours old. She had just meandered away in the night. If there were threats from animals, I could not blame her. I accepted the possibility that she was simply gone for good. It hurt, but what other choice did I have?

I could walk back to the farm, no problem. It would be a long walk, but it certainly was not impossible. I would not be able to bring my cart, though. It would be too heavy to drag back by myself, and I would have to stay on the roads to even attempt it. The stubborn part of me told myself I could handle the cart on my own. I tossed the saddle and bridle into the wagon, loaded up the five gallon bucket of water, and hooked up the nylon harness to the cart handles. My back to the harness, I strained until I started the cart rolling. It was heavy and awkward, but once it was rolling, I was able to walk at a slow, reasonable pace, dragging the thing with me. For the first mile, I told myself that this was doable. It was reasonable. I could manage this for thirty miles. I kept up that positivity until I hit the first rise in the road. I managed to get the cart halfway up the small rise on the strength of my legs and the cart's momentum, but once the momentum killed out, it was over. The cart and I reached an impasse, and the cart had a stronger will than I did. It wanted to go back to the bottom of the hill more than I wanted to crest the hill. I walked the thing back down to the bottom of the rise and parked it in the grass on the side of the road. It had taken me almost half an hour to walk a mile pulling the cart. I was sweating, exhausted, and it had been a futile act. *Stupid.*

I packed as many things as I could into my rucksack, an old Army surplus duffel, and set off on foot, my bag on my back and my shotgun carried in my hands in front of me. I felt defeated. I had spent more than a day away from Ren and the farm, I had lost our wonderful horse and the hand cart that made life so much easier, and I was walking back empty-handed. The supplies would rot in the cart, we could not get the stockade wall built, and there was nothing I could do about it. I was a failure.

It would take me at least ten hours of solid walking to get back to the farm, and that was if I could do it all without resting. Best case scenario: I would get there very late in the day. Second best scenario: I would have to camp for the night again, and get home the next day. Ren would be sick with worry, and I had no way to prevent that. The sky above was thick with roiling clouds and a storm was promising to unleash. I could not control the weather. I could not control what happened to Hera. I *could* control how I dealt with it. I started to jog, a slow, easy lope. *I'm coming, Ren. I'm coming.*

The storm hit as hard as a storm can hit. The wall cloud was many miles long, covering most of what I could see to the northwest horizon. It had slowly been approaching for the last hour, and I knew it was going to get very bad. I had only been in Texas for less than a year. I thought I had known summer squalls having lived through a few choice near-miss tornadoes in Wisconsin, but like they say: everything is bigger in Texas. Especially the storms.

As I jogged along the streets and lawns of the north side suburbs, trying to maintain a steady enough pace to eat up the miles without killing me, all the air seemed to get sucked out of the world. Everything became deathly still. The calm before the storm. I was sweating and out of breath, concentrating on my jog. I barely noticed it. Then, there was a shift in wind direction. The wind suddenly came hard out of the west, a light breeze that picked up into a harsh straight-line wind to let you know that a storm was definitely coming. It almost bowled me over when the front hit. At least the wind was cool. It felt good. I would have enjoyed it if the western sky was not positively black and foreboding.

This was not hyperbole, either. The horizon was pitch-black with a Borealis-green overtone in the clouds high above it. A long, dark curtain of dangerous incoming weather. If ever a storm wanted you to know it was dangerous, this was what it would look like. I was in the middle of a parking lot when I stopped to survey my options. I needed shelter in a hurry. If that storm produced tornadoes, which looked likely, those tornadoes had the potential to do a massive amount of damage. Seeking shelter in a large store was not the smartest thing to do. I needed a basement. I needed a tiny interior room. I needed to find a storm shelter. At the very least, I needed to find a culvert in which I could hide. Something. Anything. I paused only long enough to slug back a gulp of water from my canteen to moisten my dry mouth, and I ran for cover.

Many houses in Texas do not have basements. In Wisconsin, almost all houses have basement because the foundations have to be sunk at least six feet down, below the frost line, to make sure the foundations remain strong during the freeze/thaw cycles of the year. In southern Texas, where it rarely freezes, there are almost no basements. Why spend the money excavating a basement you don't need? They compromise by building storm shelters below the house, little cement rooms with locking doors low to the ground to keep you safe during such a potential disaster. I was able to find a storm shelter in short order by running into the nearest residential neighborhood. I had to pop the lock on the thing with a hammer and screwdriver, but it came off easily enough. I ducked into the shelter, closed and latched the doors behind me, and settled into the corner of the tiny room to wait out the worst of the storm.

I was glad to be safe, but I felt trapped and powerless. The storm raged above me and my ears filled with the sound of wind and rain. I could not help by think of the farm, exposed on the rolling prairie, with only a handful of trees to help deflect some of the straight-line wind. I hoped Ren and the baby would be safe. I hoped the animals would be safe. Wherever she was, I hoped Hera was safe. I hoped the storm would pass by the farm with a minimum of damage. No matter how much you plan, no matter how hard you work, storms are a good reminder that there is much in the world that is completely out of your control, and there's not a damned thing you can do about it. You can only accept, adjust, and continue on your path.

CHAPTER NINE

After the Storm

When the first surge of winds his the farm, I heard every building on the property groan under the stress and strength of the storm front. The winds nearly knocked me off my feet. Clutching my bulging belly with one arm and my handgun with the other, I rushed out to the barn to double-check all the doors and make sure the animals were safe in their stalls. The stalls were small and compact, and they had extra support beams overhead to strengthen them. If the barn roof should collapse or be damaged, the stalls were the safest place for the Things, pigs, and chickens. I had to battle wind and dust every step of the way. I walked leaning against the pushing winds of the front, my arm in front of my face like T.S. Lawrence in the Arabian Desert.

Satisfied that I had made the barn as structurally tight as I could, I ran back into the house and climbed into the bathtub on the first floor. It was not a storm shelter, but it was as close as I we had to one. Twist knew storms, coming from Wisconsin. Brooklyn occasionally got hit with a hurricane, but it was never truly serious, that far north. Tornadoes were something new for me. Our first month on the farm, a storm hit, a good one. Not nearly as bad as the one incoming, but bad enough. Without an actual shelter, we had laid in the bathtub together, and Twist dragged a mattress over us for extra protection. In my current state, I was in no condition to drag a mattress anywhere, so I grabbed my pile of pillows from the bed. I laid a quilt in the tub as a foundation, then put the pillows over myself. I huddled into as much of a ball as my pregnant belly would allow, and I repeated my mantra. *You will be fine. You will be fine. You will be fine.*

The baby seemed to know it was time to be quiet. He settled down. I had no idea how long the storm would take to pass, but I knew it was a bad storm, as bad as anything I had ever experienced. The winds howled and surged. The boards in the house groaned and creaked as the structure tried valiantly to stand against the storm. I heard the sound of hail and debris pinging against the vinyl siding and the loud, wooden smash of large items crashing through the yard. High above me on the second floor, the roof seemed to heave and sigh like a living thing. At one point, I felt the house stretch and yawn in the winds. I could hear the creaking groan of wood on nails. The walls shook and shimmied.

What would we do if the storm took down this house? Would we just go find another one? What of the food we planted? What of the animals? I understood at that moment why family farms existed for generations. The idea of moving everything and finding a new spot seemed overwhelming, not to mention I really *loved* this farm. I loved everything about it. I loved the thought of raising my baby here. I loved that this was *mine*. Well, *ours*. I couldn't say we bought it, but we certainly owned it now. I don't think anyone would argue with us when we said it was "ours." My parents had always rented, first the tiny apartment over the deli in Brooklyn, and then a larger apartment in a tall apartment complex, and then the row house where they were now buried in the little backyard. They had never "owned" a home. I owned this farm. I was willing to fight for this plot of land. I was willing to give it my blood, sweat, and tears. But, what could I do against a tornado?

The front seemed to rage for hours. I could not sleep, as tired as I was. I could not eat, hungry as I was. I have no idea how long the storm actually lasted, but I knew it was too long. A lifetime passed while I lay in that bathtub. Then, as if the storm decided to say, "Only joking!" the winds died to a gentle tailing breeze behind the front, and the only sound was the heavy, steady tattoo of rain. I breathed a long sigh of relief and pulled myself out of the bathtub to start a survey of the damage.

I was not mentally prepared for the amount of damage the storm had done to the farm, but at the same time, I was grateful it was not worse. Two tall birch trees had fallen at the edge of the property. They were total losses, but could be cut apart for firewood. There would be enough wood there for a couple months' worth of cooking and heat. I thought of Caroline Ingalls in the "Little House" books. She always said that there was no great loss without some gain. Maybe she was right. The house was mostly intact. A few panels of siding had ripped away and gone who-knows-where. There was plenty of pockmarks from things hitting the siding, but that was only cosmetic. I don't know if there is any sort of "fix" for that, but I can grow to love pockmarks, if necessary. Of the twenty-two solar panels on the roof of the house, barn, and array in the yard next to the house, at least six were missing entirely—whisked away to Oz. Mainly the ones on the barn roof. Another six were cracked or damaged beyond repair. It would certainly cut into the power generation for the house. That hurt. It put dreams of having refrigeration and a washing machine on the back-burner once again. They would have to be replaced. I had no idea how many spares Twist had stashed in the garage of the "store" house, but I would leave that to him.

The yard where we spent most of our time was a disaster of tree limbs, debris, and muddy ground. It could be cleaned up, but it would take some time and labor. We had all the time in the world, but I was in no condition to provide labor. That would have to be Twist's project. Some of our cooking supplies we kept in the backyard had been scattered around. I could clean that up, easily enough. The garden was a different matter. Most of the corn plants were flattened. All of the above-ground plants, with the exception of the low-to-the-ground plants, like lettuce and cabbage, were wrecked. Even the lettuce and cabbage didn't look healthy anymore. Their outer leaves were ragged and torn. Their round centers were roughed up. I could save a lot of the food. Some of it could be eaten in the next couple of days. Some of it could be dried or pickled. Some of it was a complete loss, though. The root vegetables would be fine. The berry bushes on the edges of the property did not look like they incurred too much damage. We would make do.

My biggest concern was the barn. The barn was every bit as important as the house. I knew right away that something was wrong when I looked to the barn and saw Thing 1 and three of the pigs staring at me from the large square of space where a pair of sliding doors should have been. Thing 2, the rest of the pigs, and a lot of the chickens were elsewhere. I called for the cow and the pigs, but they were nowhere nearby.

I felt a hard twinge in my lower abdomen again, like a hard poke with something sharp. It took my breath away. *Not now, kiddo.* I needed to eat something, but I had no desire to do so. I needed to have some water, too. I needed to start cleaning the yard. A large wave of hormone-influence emotion crashed over me. I felt tears start to prick at my eyes. I felt fear, sadness, and defeat all at once. It took everything I had not to collapse in the wet mud and grass and cry. I was not going to give the storm the satisfaction, though. It may have taken something from us, but it did not take everything.

We could easily rebuild. We still had some of our animals. Hardships must be endured. I would endure. *My family would endure.*

I sniffed hard and bit the side of my tongue with my molars. The pain sharpened my focus and made the tears stop. Crying was not going to make everything magically repair itself. That would only be done through hard work, and I was the only one who could do it now.

I went back in the house to change into clothes I did not mind getting muddy. As I changed, I caught sight of myself in the full-length mirror on the back of the bedroom door. I was a house. I was a planet. My body looked like a funhouse-mirror version of myself. Where once I was petite and slim with gentle curves, I was a Silly Putty-stretched caricature of my former self. My breasts were at least three times their former size. They reminded me of my mother's. My butt was flattened and wide, my hips splayed to a comical degree, and my stomach bulged out in front of me to unfathomable proportions. I could rest a teacup and saucer on the top of my belly. I was a clown. Worse than a clown. I was Grimace from the old McDonald's commercials, just paint me purple and give me a milkshake. That hormone-fueled melancholy hit me again. I was mourning who I used to be instead of looking to the future. *Get a hold of yourself, girl.* It wasn't worth holding a funeral for a body that was doing exactly what it was meant to do. People change. Things change. Bodies change. Get used to it.

I tugged on pair of maternity jeans, the soft, stretchy waistband wrapping high on my belly. I pulled on a caftan-like sweatshirt of Twist's. I slipped my feet into my tennis shoes because I could not bear to bend down to tie my boots anymore. I grabbed leather gloves to protect my hands, and I got to work.

The first order of business was securing the barn door that had blown away. I could see where the wind tossed the door, maybe fifty yards from the barn. It was lying flat in some taller grass. The majority of the door looked unharmed. Only the rolling wheels on the top where it slipped into the pipe above the door were missing, and they were probably still in the pipe. There was no way I was going to lift that door and drag it back into place, so I got a hammer and a box of four-inch nails. One by one, I dragged two-by-fours from the stack in the garage and hammered them into place to make a temporary door. I spaced them about eight or ten inches apart, hammering the nail mostly into place on one side, then going to the other and driving it into the other side. It wasn't pretty, but it would work. When Twist came home, he could make it pretty again.

If he comes home, whispered the evil part of my brain. I cursed that thought and continued to work. It took me a dozen trips to the barn to make a functional barrier that would keep Thing 1 and the pigs in and predators out. When I spied a rogue chicken wandering around the yard, I would shoo them into the barn. I put them in a stall and closed the door. It would serve as a temporary arrangement to keep them safe and confined. The storm had torn apart the front half of the cage I used for their grazing area, which was how they escaped. It would be a simple enough repair, but it would be a repair for another day. For now, there was too much else to do.

When I secured the barn to the best of my ability, I was soaked to the skin from the rain, so I was both freezing cold from the water, and sweating from my labor. My back was hurting like nothing I've ever known before. The muscles along my spine felt constricted, like little clenched fists. I tried to rub the pain away, but couldn't. I took a couple deep breaths and forced myself to ignore the pain. *Other women have had it far worse than you,* I reminded myself.

I set about gathering up food from the destroyed plants. The sweet corn was a ripe enough that I could eat some that day, and then dry the rest when the sun came back. The ears that were not salvageable went to the pigs. I picked the pods from the wrecked pea plants. I picked green tomatoes from broken vines. It was slow work, bent over at the waist or crouched on swollen calves. The baby did not care for his home to be so constricted and protested with a flurry of Tae Kwon Do kicks to my lungs and bladder. *Thanks, kid.* I told him that if he didn't knock it off, he would be grounded until he was twelve. He did not seem to comprehend and kept fighting me every time I had to bend at the waist. Not even born, and already he's disobedient. I'm not going to win Mom of the Year.

I did what I could with the garden. I Ziploc-bagged some of the fresh stuff and stored it in the dark cupboards in the house. The clock was ticking on them. They would have to be eaten quickly. I stacked the rest on the counters to wait for the rain to stop so I could dry them outside. What could be pickled was piled on the counter to wait for tomorrow. I would get a vat of pickling brine and some of the mason jars I had in the garage. It would not be perfect, but it would have to do. When the food was secure, I then went looking for Thing 2 and the missing pigs.

The rain was still coming down steadily. It wasn't heavy, but it was constant. I changed into dry clothes, grabbed a golf umbrella from the closet, and a walking stick Twist had carved and sanded smooth for me one night by the fire. It helped to have something to lean on when I was going up and down the little hills in the area. I could not buckle my gun belt around my waist, so I set it as large as I could make it and slipped it around my head and arm like a bandolier, the gun resting in its holster on the shelf my belly made.

I trudged through the knee-high grass past the barn calling for Thing 2 and making that silly high-pitched "soooo-ee!" call that Twist used when he fed the pigs. I had thought that doing that was a Hollywood thing, made up for movies and TV. But, the pigs actually responded to it. Every time he did that, they came charging. He said that pigs were as smart as dogs, and that they learned to identify the noise with being fed. It was like how dogs and cats responded to electric can openers or the crinkle of heavy foil bags.

After ten minutes of walking and calling, I found one of the smaller pigs, a hairy little white pig I called James MacAvoy. *(I named all the pigs after movie stars I used to like.)* I could not put a leash on him and continue searching for the others, so I had to walk him back to the barn and put him with his friends, Michael Fassbender, Scarlett Johannson, Dame Helen Mirren, and Tina Fey. I was still missing Amy Poehler (who looked a lot like Tina Fey, but had lighter hair), and Keira Knightley (who was *really* thin when we first found her). The lion killed Christian Bale, if you were wondering. Poor, poor Christian Bale.

When MacAvoy was secured, I went back to walking and calling. My back became tighter and tighter. I could not seem to get comfortable. I felt a little sick, probably from not eating enough that day, and I was a little light-headed, probably from dehydration. I should have brought some supplies, but it wasn't like I was going out on a three-day hike. I was just walking the property. If I found them, I found them. If I didn't, I didn't. I would go back to the house after an hour or two. *Walking is good for pregnant women,* I reminded myself. *Toughen up.*

The rain drummed on the umbrella steadily. The grass soaked my jeans and the denim wicked the water higher up on my thighs. My skin started to chafe uncomfortably. I tried to ignore it for at least a mile, but between my thighs, which I knew were getting dangerously raw, and my back, which I knew would be projecting me into a new world of agony later that night, I had to cut my losses and go home. The pigs and Thing 2 would stay lost for now. Maybe they would come home. Maybe they wouldn't. I tried my best. My body was sore and aching. My belly hurt. Cradling my enormous gut, I limped back to the house. I had done what I could. I needed to eat, drink, and most importantly—rest.

CHAPTER TEN

My Kingdom for a Bike

It was nearly dark by the time the storm passed. The sky was gray and the post-storm sunlight filtering through the clouds gave the world a strange, flat look. The sun was nearly below the horizon; that had something to do with it. I left the sanctuary of the storm shelter to a world of chaos. I did not believe that a tornado hit; the wind was not swirling. It had been a straight-line wind, but the initial winds had been strong enough to remind me of a tornado's power. When I poked my head out of the cellar, I saw downed trees and damaged houses everywhere. None of the damage was extreme, save for the one or two houses that had been unlucky enough to have a tree fall on them, but it was enough to make me give a low whistle. My thoughts were solely on the farm. How bad was it there? I was still at least twenty, maybe twenty-five miles from home. It was still raining. There was nothing I could do but resume walking. I stopped long enough to find a poncho to minimize the saturation from the storm, but by the time I found one, the damage was done. I was soaked.

I walked about four blocks in the rain before I realized I

was being stupid. I could just find a bike. They were in practically every garage. After two years, all the tires in the world were flat, but that could easily be remedied with a good, old-fashioned hand pump. Those...were surprisingly not as easy to find. Many people had transitioned to electric pumps. The electric pumps were no help to me at the moment. Back at the house, with the solar power, they might be acceptable. However, in the wasteland they were essentially a rock with extra wiring. A bike would do me no good with flat tires, so I needed to find a pump first. Considering I was waist-deep in the suburbs, there had to be one somewhere. It would just take some wrangling. I had to start breaking into garages.

Given that most garages in the modern era were electric and controlled by remotes, it wasn't like I could just walk up and start yanking doors. I had to break into the houses, first. Then, I had to get to the garage, disengage the garage door from electric to manual, and then search through the garage for what I needed. This seems like it's not that big of a deal, right? Well, you would be wrong. For some reason, about every third or fourth home treated their garage like a storage locker. Anytime I saw a house with two or three cars in the driveway, I knew the garage was stockpiled with boxes, old furniture, CRT monitors and old-style TVs, and all matter of other junk that they would have been better off just getting rid of at some point. Those types of people were not true "hoarders," *per se* — but they certainly had an issue. Their houses were clean and uncluttered, just the garage was a pile of junk. I'm sure those people would have been mortified to open the garage doors and let the neighbors see their piles of junk. Those garages were impossible to even enter, let alone find a bicycle pump in them. Now, considering a lot of people did not die at home when the Flu hit, I did not always know to not bother with a house because of the cars in the driveway.

I went to the nearest house, one of those nondescript cookie-cutter bland, beige homes that populated every post-1980 suburb in America, and tried the garage door. It was, of course, locked. I knew it would be, but it was always worth giving it a try. The next step was to try the doors. The front door was locked, but the sliding patio door on the raised deck behind the house was unlocked. It slid open easily, and I took a light blast of stale death-smell to the face. The house was the final resting place for one, maybe more people. I flipped on the flashlight I always carried in my bag. It was a simple, nondescript house in a basic layout. The deck led to a small dining area, kitchen to the left, a living room straight ahead. I saw a body on the floor of the living room. No, two. A child's body was on the couch, covered in a blanket. Next to the child, on the floor, was an adult. They were mummified from Texas heat and dry air. A small dog was curled on the floor next to them, thin and gaunt. The little dog, trapped inside, had starved to death watching over his unresponsive family. This made me think of Rowdy, my neighbor's dog who became my dog until his death back in Wisconsin. The sudden rush of emotion made my eyes sting. *Good dog.*

I tried to ignore the bodies, shutting the sliding door behind me. I went into the garage and found a typical garage: a single car on one side, and bikes, lawn mower, and a kayak on the other. All the tires on the vehicles were flat. I poked around looking for a pump. No dice. I had to move on to the next house.

I moved to the next house, and then the house after that one. At the fourth house, I stopped. The house had a full array of solar panels on the roof. They looked like they were in good condition. This house could actually have power. That was worth investigating on its own.

I moved to the garage door and tried it. Locked. The front door, also locked. I moved around to the rear of the house. Like most of the houses in the neighborhood, there was a large rear yard with an elevated wooden deck. I could see the sliding patio door, but this house had a balcony-style deck with no staircase. There was a basement door in the corner of the house next to a small, brick patio on the ground. I moved to that door and tried it. Locked. When the doors thwarted my efforts, my only option was to use tools to force the door. I was practiced in this by now. Over the last two years, I had defeated hundreds of locks, some by finesse, and some by force. I used a screwdriver from my ruck to force the lock, twisting it until I felt it slip past the tumblers. It wasn't a perfect solution, and it would break the lock more often than not, but it worked. I heard the metal crunch, and I felt the door pop open. I slipped into the house and flipped on the flashlight.

Immediately, I froze. The entire basement of the house looked like a doomsday prepper's how-to guide. There were nothing but floor-to-ceiling plastic shelves loaded with supplies: canned goods, bottled water, soft drinks, vacuum-sealed bags of dried meat and vegetables, toilet paper, Wet Wipes, boxes of cereal and other dry goods. It was a storehouse. I had run into these before, people who prepared for war or a chemical attack or something similar, only to succumb to a virus, something they could not even see or fight. I made a mental note to remember the address of this house and come back to it, when I could.

I slipped around the racks and moved toward the staircase. I trotted up the stairs, preparing to find just another abandoned house. When I got to the top of the stairs and turned to enter a kitchen, three things happened at once: I saw a shadow, I heard an explosion, and I felt like a hive of wasps decided to attack my left hip.

I realized that I was flat on my back in the little landing at the top of the stairs. I was stunned. I saw stars. *How? Where? Why?* I couldn't breathe. There was stinging, nasty pain everywhere. My left side was on fire. I clapped my hand to my hip and felt warm wetness. I was bleeding.

"Oh…oh! Jeez. I'm sorry. I didn't mean to pull the trigger! That was an accident!" A man's voice? A boy's voice? Someone was apologizing to me. My vision got blurry, hazy.

I was shot. Someone shot me. Who would shoot me? I heard movement. The next thing I knew, I felt pressure on my hip. I could feel the rough texture of paper towels. Someone was trying to stop the bleeding.

Getting shot was not like it was in the movies. In the movies, the hero gets shot, he grimaces in a manly fashion, and he continues on as if a bullet was a minor annoyance like stepping on a Lego or getting stung by a bee. I could feel blood seeping down my thigh, and down my side to pool at the small of my back. Was it a lot of blood? I couldn't tell. I felt a cold shudder ripple through my body. Shock. I was definitely shocked. I had not been expecting anything to happen when I turned that corner.

"Dude, I'm sorry," the man was saying again. His voice was higher-pitched, squeaky, almost. He sounded panicked. That could account for the squeak. "I just meant to point the gun and tell you not to move, but...I don't know what happened. I screwed up. Aw, geez. Don't die, okay. Just don't die."

"Die?" I heard myself say. I wasn't going to die. I had to get back to the farm. I had a baby coming, and he would need a father. "I'm not going to die." My voice came out odd and wispy. I was losing consciousness. A light blazed on overhead, a real light. A ceiling lamp in a kitchen. It blinded me. I blinked to try to make my eyes dilate. After a long moment, I could see a shadow above me.

"I'm gonna fix you up real good. Just stay with me."

I could make out a wild mop of blond, curly hair. I saw a hunched figure, slightly chubby. He had a thick, wild beard and he was wearing glasses with heavy black frames. He was also wearing a Command Gold uniform jersey from the original Star Trek TV show.

CHAPTER ELEVEN

Panthera Leo

The sound of screaming woke me from a nightmare. Was the screaming in my nightmare, or was it coming from outside? I couldn't tell. I couldn't even remember the nightmare, but I knew it was a nightmare. I felt attacked. I felt punchy, almost drunk in a way. Something was wrong. I was wrong. The baby? My hand went to my stomach instinctively. The baby couldn't be screaming. I heard the sound again. It was coming from outside. The pigs. One pig? More pigs? I couldn't tell.

A pregnant woman does not just "spring" out of bed, no matter how badly she wants to. Getting out of bed was a multi-stage process. I had to get my feet under me, make sure they could support my weight and balance, and then move to standing, using the headboard to help me propel myself to my feet. From there, I grabbed my gun, my flashlight, slipped my feet into my sneakers, and waddled down the stairs and out of the house as fast as I could, which was not very fast at all. The whole time, I could hear the sound of animals in distress. It was chilling.

When I threw open the door to the yard, it was morning.

The rain had stopped, but the whole world was misty with thin fog and dawn light. I could see the barn, seventy yards across the lawn. The boards I nailed across the opening were still there. I could see the shadows of moving animals beyond them in the dark of the arena. The pigs were still okay. Thing 1 was still okay. I heard more screaming. It was coming from the other side of the barn.

One of the missing pigs had come home and was trying to get into shelter, I thought. That was hardly something to fuss over. I moved around the corner of the barn to the field behind it and saw Keira Knightley squealing and sprinting like a crazed rabbit, a large, tawny lion trying to chase her down. Keira's little legs were churning like cartoon animal's and she was shifting direction often, keeping the heavier, less shifty lion guessing. The lion was gaining. She would get a little distance and rush back to the barn door, where she knew there was safety. When she got to the door that did not open, the lion would charge her again, and she would start over from the beginning.

I hate to say it, but I froze. I know what I should have done, shooting at the lion, or at least shooting into the air to try to scare it away, but I didn't, not at first. I froze and froze hard. To see a fully-grown lion less than fifty yards from me, with no fences or walls between us, it was terrifying. A cold sweat burst out over my body. The gun in my hand became ten times heavier. I felt a tremble rip through my body. I almost peed my pants (*my bladder control was already questionable thanks to the pregnancy*). I felt my heart race. I was not prepared for an animal of that size and strength to be this close to me.

And then I felt the baby kick me. Hard. It was almost as if the little pisher was telling me to get my act in gear. I don't know how to explain it, other than to say it was that mythical "Mama Bear" instinct kicking in. That pig was *my* pig. I had been feeding her, petting her, and making sure she was healthy for months. I felt a weird, protective instinct descend over me. That pig. My baby. At that moment, there was no difference between the two. That pig *was* my baby, and to hell with any lion that thinks he was going to eat my baby.

A strange force possessed my arm. I went full Dirty Harry on this lion. I yanked the gun up to a firing position, widened my stance, sighted down the barrel with my right eye, and started calmly squeezing off rounds. I had practiced with this pistol, and I liked to think I was a decent shot. I saw two puffs of red as my bullets found their target, burying into the left side of the lion's rump. The big cat snarled and deviated from its pursuit course. I hit it again on the right side as it turned. The cat, annoyed and confused, decided to cut its losses and run. Angry, I continued to fire at it, but I don't think I hit it again. I squeezed off rounds until the hammer clicked on empty air.

Keira Knightley was scared and trembling, a quartet of large, bloody slashes across her backside. She was huddled by the door, desperate to find safety with her friends. I let her into the barn and got the first aid kit to treat her wounds. I was halfway back to the barn when I realized I wasn't breathing. I had to stop and suck in a deep lungful of air. The baby twitched hard, and the sudden, sharp pain doubled me over. I put my hands on my knees and bore the pain until it passed. For a fleeting second, I worried that I was having a contraction, but it was still too early for that.

Wasn't it?

No. I would not allow this baby to be born until Twist returned. We had at least two months before it was due. It was just a reaction to the gunfire and my own nerves. When the pain passed, I felt fine. It was just a fetal temper-tantrum. I had a pig to treat, and chores to do. No time for pain or worry. The storm was past, the sun was rising, and I needed to busy myself lest I dwell on why Twist hasn't returned.

CHAPTER TWELVE

Chet

The man in the gold Trek costume helped drag me to my feet. I could not put weight on my left leg. My hip was burning. It felt wrecked, as if all the bones on the left side of my pelvis had been turned into Play-doh. I had fleeting visions of a wheelchair. How could I help Ren around the farm if I couldn't walk? The panic started my heart racing.

"Keep cool, man. Keep cool. You'll be fine." The chubby guy swept a bunch of papers and garbage from a large table in the dining room. I rolled onto the table. "It's just a flesh wound!" he mimicked a bad British accent. The guy turned on the light over the table, and I had to close my eyes. It was bright, too bright.

"I'm gonna get some stuff to fix you up. Man, I apologize. I didn't mean to shoot, honest to God, I didn't. It was dark, and I got twitchy. I'm not a violent guy, honest."

"S'ok." My mouth felt cottony. I felt him cutting down the leg of my pants from the hip. I felt the fiery brush of gauze on the wound. It helped to keep me alert.

"Well, that's not too bad." The man in the Star Trek uniform smiled at me. "Thankfully, I'm a lousy shot on the best of days. You'll live, Slippery. Looks like a really nasty road rash, is all." He packed a wad of gauze onto my side and told me to hold it in place. He rooted around in a large tackle box loaded with bandages, creams, salves, and suture kits. He took out a bottle of rubbing alcohol and poured it on my side. I screamed. He sympathized with me. "I bet that burns like hell, don't it?" He had a very distinct east-Texas drawl.

"Who are you?" I had to speak through gritted teeth. The PSI I was using to wrench my jaw shut threatened to pop my teeth like bubble wrap.

"Name's Charles. People call me Chet, though. My old man was Charles, and my mom didn't like the name Charlie or Junior, so I became Chet. Pleased to meet you."

"I'm Twist."

"Twist? Like the verb?"

"Short for Twister."

"Did your parents not like you?"

"Nickname from wrestling in high school."

"And you just call yourself that? Cool, I guess." Chet scrubbed at the wound with more gauze. I was becoming numb to the pain. "It looks like the slug took a nice chunk of meat off your side, but you'll be fine. You'll be limpin' for a while, but you'll recover."

"Good to know."

"This is gonna bleed like a mother for a while, though. Sorry about that." Chet rinsed the wound with alcohol again. Then, he smeared a salve over it. It must have had lidocaine in it, because the pain reduced considerably. For the first time in minutes, I took an easy breath. Chet packed on a large bandage, the kind they used in the military to stop bleeding. He taped it down with white medical tape and stood back to survey his work. "You'll live," he repeated.

"I have to get home."

"It's dark out, man. You ain't goin' nowhere for a while."

"I have to get home—"

Chet cut me off. "It ain't safe after dark. There's dogs, 'yotes, and crazy fools with guns. I swear I've heard wolves, too. Must have escaped from a zoo or something. You can stay here with me, though. Be glad for the company, really. It's all good. I've got power, water, and food. We can make a cheeseless pizza, if you want. Ain't had real cheese around here in months. I got some frozen stuff, but not much. Want to watch some 'X-Files' or maybe some 'Firefly?' How long has it been since you can say you watched TV?"

Chet helped me to sit up. My hip did not want to work properly. Remind me to never get shot again. With Chet acting like a human crutch, he helped me off the table and to a book and paper-cluttered couch. He swept the papers away to clear a space for me. For the first time, I was able to see where I was. It was a very nice, if nondescript house, but every square inch of the place seemed packed with books, papers, sci-fi memorabilia, and electronic parts. In between the hoarder-like mess was survival gear like water and stacks of canned food. It was a lot to take in, at first. The house was busy. In every direction, there was something to see.

"Sorry about shooting you, brother." Chet handed me a bottle of cold water he retrieved from the working refrigerator in the kitchen. It was such a treat to have cold, clean water, I drained the bottle in a single breath. Chet got me another. "No hard feelings, right?" He stuck out his hand.

"No hard feelings." We shook.

"Honestly, man—I just meant to point the gun at you to hold you until I could determine if you were gonna be cool or not. You seem like a good guy, though."

"Thanks. I like to think I am."

"You're not all gonna be shooting me, or taking my stuff, are you?"

"No. Not at all."

"Well, all right then. Cool." He smiled. Then he squinted at me. "Wait, are you just saying you won't so I drop my guard, but you're planning to shoot me later?"

I shook my head. I pointed toward where I dropped my shotgun in the stairwell. "I had a gun. I could have used it to shoot you after you shot me."

"Fair enough." Chet ran a hand through his shaggy mane. "It's just hard to know who to trust, you know what I mean?"

"I get that."

"You want to be nice and neighborly, help everyone, you know? But, you never know who's going to be in that alpha-dog survival mode and want to shoot it out rather than shaking hands, eh?"

I nodded at the stacks of survival supplies in the corners. "You look like you're doing okay."

Chet shrugged. "I guess I am. I'm luckier than most, I suppose. Not that there's all that many of us left. I had time to prepare, though."

"You had time to prepare for the Flu?"

Chet shrugged again, like it was no big deal. Like he wasn't just changing my understanding of the global-killer virus that decimated humanity. "Yeah. More than most, I guess."

"What? How? By the time people were realizing the Flu had hit, there was like four or five weeks, and everyone was dead. I had to start from scratch. I had to start with almost nothing."

"That's what I mean. Most people, they only knew when the bodies started dropping." Chet pointed at a computer in the corner. "I was a big nerd, if you couldn't tell from looking around. I was a computer programmer and a minor hacker of little renown. I was on the Dark Web a long time ago when I started reading rumors about some sort of super virus. I could never lock down the definite, hard truth about it, but I knew enough to know that there was something out there. It was never a question of *if* it would be released, but *when* it would be released. Something bad was coming, that much was evident for those of us who knew to look for it."

What? What was this guy trying to say? "Are you saying the Flu was manufactured? That man killed itself with some sort of genetically altered virus?"

Chet nodded. "Best I can figure, yeah. From what I gathered, I'd say that's about right. I will never know for certain, of course, but I'd be willing to bet a pretty high amount on it."

I felt my jaw hanging open. I was floored. "Tell me more. What do you know?"

"Not that much, honestly. And, I can't truly verify anything I think I know, so I might be full of it. Who knows? But anyway, the Flu hit hard in early May two years and a few months ago, right? Say, two-and-a-half years." Chet cleared some books off a wooden dining room chair and sat on it, facing me. "About a year before that, I was on a pretty secretive conspiracy chat room, way down the rabbit hole, right? I was totally looking for Morpheus' red pill. Most of the time, the chatter in those sorts of chatrooms is pretty dumb: aliens, exorcisms, politics, lizard people—useless idiocy, for the most part. Well, one night, I'm on there and a guy gets on and starts typing stuff out in bad, broken English. Says he was a Chinese soldier guarding some sort of top-secret, hidden genetics lab somewhere in some remote part of China. He starts talking about how their scientists made some sort of wicked chemical weapon. At first, I think it's B.S. because how could he get past the Great Firewall of China, right?"

I knew next-to-nothing about computers, so I just nodded like I understood.

Chet continued. "He's really insistent, though. Says they were testing this aerosolized virus that could be administered to a primate, and then it basically turned that ape into a walking infection agent for a month before killing it. I guess they had a cure for it at first, but the chemically-altered virus mutated beyond the cure in about a month's time. Then, the guy disappears from the chatroom for a week. When he comes back, he says that he's been infected, that everyone in the lab has been infected, and that the virus is unstoppable."

"Unless you're immune."

Chet's eyebrows raised. He gave a low whistle. "You're immune?"

"I guess. I never really got sick in my life, and when everyone else died, I stayed alive. That sounds like immunity to me."

"Man, I get sick *a lot*. Bad allergies. Frequent colds. My mom threated to make me live in a plastic bubble when I was a kid."

"So, how did you survive?"

"Luck, mostly." Chet's gaze jumped to the window behind the couch where I sat. For the first time, I noticed that it was covered with a thick sheet of plastic, the kind of heavy-duty plastic people in Wisconsin used to cover windows and patio doors for the winter to help with heating bills. "I figured this guy was on the level. His story seemed too real to be completely B.S. He had data. He had specifics. He had a few video clips of dead apes. It was either real, or one of the greatest hoaxes ever made. I figured something bad was coming, so I quit my job. I cashed in all my investments, sold my car—the works. I liquidated everything I could, and then I converted my house in about a month. Paid top dollar for companies to come in a drop everything to get my house off the grid. Solar. Water. Sewer. The works, really. I had them all bill me later, knowing full well I'd never have to pay them. That's sort of a bad trick, but I figured I was saving my life, right?"

"What if the Flu hadn't hit?"

Chet laughed. "I was prepared to jump off that bridge when I came to it. I was really good with computers, worse came to worst, I would have sold the house to pay my bills and rebuilt my nut in the dot-coms somehow. Everyone needed a coder, you know. If you can program, you can work. That's the way of the computer world. I would have been okay one way or another."

"So, you built a bunker, essentially."

"I did. Made the house as virus-proof as I could, and then I prepared it for the collapse of society. I stocked this place with all the food and water that it could hold. I bought extra freezers and loaded them with frozen pizzas and other things that would be easy to make. I sealed the doors and windows, cut myself off to the outside world. Then, I just waited. I read the news out of China, Hong Kong, and Singapore every day. I waited to see reports of epidemics. Once they started, I knew the world was done for. It was about a two-month bleed from the initial reports of the first deaths to the Big Empty we have now."

Something horrifying occurred to me. I clapped a hand to my mouth. "And I just infected you, didn't I?"

Chet waved off my concern. "Nah. Virus had a real short life. It either killed its host or died inside it in about thirty days. With no more primates to kill, the virus died. The Flu is gone from this world, I'm pretty sure. Anyone born now will survive. I'm not worried anymore. I've been out and about a bunch now. I lived. So did you, apparently. There are a few more of us out there, too."

"I found some nice Latinos a few streets over—"

"Enrique and his people? They do some trading with me occasionally. Good folks."

"Yeah. They were nice. Fair."

"There are a couple of rogue factions in Houston. You might want to steer clear of the downtown areas. From what Enrique and his crew tell me, I hear it's a minor war zone."

"Thanks for the advice."

"More people are coming, too. Houston is about to become a civilization hub. People are moving south. They're heading for metropolitan areas with land, access to the ocean, access to freshwater inland, a long growing season, and high potential for solar energy."

"How do you know this?"

Chet stood. He held out a hand to help me to my feet. "Are you well enough to limp?"

I could see blood staining the bandage on my hip, but the pain was minimal. I wasn't in great shape, but I could deal with it. "Yeah. I can make it."

Chet walked me to a small, cluttered study down the hall. Where once a computer would have taken the center-spot on a desk, there was instead a small contraption of wires and diodes and dials. A large, old-timey radio-style microphone sat in front of it. "Ham radio. About the only thing that works anymore. It was my old man's. After he died, it was in a box in the basement. I found it when I started stockpiling food. Figured it might come in handy. There are other people out there with radios, Twist. Not a ton of 'em, but enough that it gives me some hope that humanity might recover someday. Someday well into the future."

Chet sat down at the radio and pressed his face to the microphone. He flipped some switches and the radio hummed to life. "Attention out there in Radio Land. Who is listening tonight? This is Captain Kirk coming to you from the great state of Texas. If you can hear me, come back."

Chet fiddled with the dials for a moment. I heard the familiar hiss and pop of radio static. Then, a voice wafted out of the speakers, thin and distant, but definitely human. "Hey, Cap'n Kirk! Good to hear someone's voice again. This is Special Wilderness Agent Jethro Tully out of Cook City, Montana."

"Hey, Mr. Tully! Good to hear you're still alive. You ain't been made into bear food, yet."

"Not for lack of trying. Them sumbitches are getting' ornery. What's the good word out of Houston tonight?"

Chet gestured for me to get closer to the mic. "Found another brave soul in the night. Tully, this is Twist." Chet motioned for me to talk.

I cleared my throat. "Uh...hello. Nice to hear your voice, Mr. Tully."

"Call me Jethro. What kind of a name is Twist? Did your parents not like you?"

"It's a nickname," I said. "What kind of a name is Jethro Tully? Do you have an Aqualung?"

"It's just a radio handle, m'boy. Real name is Marty Tambour."

Chet took over the mic again. "Any news from the north?"

"Nothing new, no. Saw a couple of Canadians riding south on horseback a few weeks ago, loaded with gear. They said they were heading to where it was warm. I told them to head for Houston and to look you up when they got there."

"I'll keep an eye out for them. Hopefully, they don't run into the idiots shooting each other downtown."

Tully sighed. "Pretty sad, that. Only a few thousand of us left, and those idiots got to shoot each other over nothing."

"Well, keep me posted, J.T. I think me and Twist are gonna watch some DVDs or something."

"Sounds like a plan. Wish I could join you. Jethro, out."

"Captain Kirk, out." Chet signed off the radio. He clicked the microphone switch to off. "There you go. People are still alive."

"He's in Montana?"

"Yeah. I told him he should come south, but he's elderly. Says he'll stay where he is until he dies."

"I moved away from Wisconsin because the winters are too harsh."

Chet nodded sagely. "That's why people are moving south. Houston is going to become a new hotbed of civilization. A couple of the cities in central Florida have some growth. A couple of California cities, too. Los Angeles and San Francisco, of course, but also a few smaller cities in the north are getting populated."

"Do you have any idea how many people survived?"

Chet shook his head. "Not an accurate count, no. Only a really rough guess. I figure, given the people I've been able to communicate with on the radio, and the people I've been able to track around Houston, using a rough mathematical estimate, I figure somewhere around twenty-thousand people survived. Maybe as high as thirty or forty. But that's a really, really rough guess, mind you. I might be way off."

"Twenty-thousand? Maybe thirty or forty? In the US?"

Chet's face looked sad. He shook his head again. "Twenty-thousand worldwide. In the US, it's probably less than ten thousand, best guess. The math gets sketchy overseas. I have not talked to too many people around the world. There's a guy in Brisbane, Australia who said that the major cities were wiped out, but a bunch of those crazy guys in the Outback were still alive, thanks to a lack of human contact. That might be true for some of the more remote parts of the world, too. I imagine there might be entire villages in Laos or Vietnam or something like that where no one in the village ever left, and no one visited the major metropolitan areas to get infected. As long as migrating monkeys didn't bring the virus into their village, there might be entire villages that survived unscathed, but most of those towns are probably pretty Third-World, so they aren't exactly contacting people by radio." Chet patted the microphone of his ham radio. "I doubt too many people left in the world thought to bust out this old tech. I'm amazed by the number who did, though. This system still works, even though everything else doesn't. Marconi knew what he was doing with this stuff, didn't he?"

I wasn't sure who Marconi was, so I just nodded again. "True."

"Crazy stuff, ain't it?" Chet slumped in a chair. "One day, we're all in the rat race, just tryin' to make some cheddar, and the next, the race is over, we've lost, and we're scrappin' for crumbs."

I was amazed that Chet had been so far ahead of everyone on the Flu. I wondered how many other "prepper" types out there had been on the same chat rooms. My head was also swimming with the notion of Houston becoming a new

Cradle of Civilization. There were already people in the city, dozens apparently, and more were coming. I thought of the farm. Would people want to live there? Could I afford to let them? Could I afford to turn them away? Should I stay hidden as best I could?

"People think you're crazy when you start broadcasting gloom-and-doom forecasts, until those forecasts come true, I guess." Chet shook his head. "Usually, by then, the shit has hit the fan, and we're all screwed-blue and tattooed. Game over."

"I need to get home." I tried to stand, but my hip still didn't want to work. Around the wound site, the skin and muscle was swelling badly.

Chet gave a low whistle again. "You ain't goin' anywhere for a while, *mon frer*. Let me get you a Cold-pak for that hip." He retreated from the radio room and returned with one of those dry-storage cold packs. He popped the chemical pack inside and shook the bag for a few seconds. When he handed it to me, it was already pleasantly cold. I set it on my hip, just below the wound-site.

"I have a wife."

Chet's eyebrows raised. "You do? Rock on. You look awfully young to be married, but I guess that don't matter much anymore, eh? Age is nothin' but a number, right?"

"She was expecting me back yesterday. I need to get back to her. I need to get home."

"That's rough, man. I sympathize. You ain't going to be up for traveling for a few days, though. There's not much I can do about it, either. You're going to be fine, but you need to rest. You can hang out here, though. Least I can do after I shot you and all. And I'll be glad for the company."

I shook my head. "No. I appreciate the offer, but I really need to get back there. Do you have a bike I can ride?"

"You ain't ridin' no bikes for a while. Think about it. You can't even stand on that leg, let alone push down on a pedal."

He was right. My plan to cycle back home was now null

and void. "Crutches, then? Do you have crutches?"

"How far away do you live from here?"

I told him the truth and a lie. "About twenty-five, thirty miles northwest of here."

"And you think you're going to crutch there? Dude, your armpits would be hash by the time you get there."

They would be. I knew this. I sprained my ankle wrestling during my sophomore year, and I was on crutches for three weeks. Limping around on sticks like that is hard on your tender parts under your arms. You need time to toughen the skin and build up callouses. That did not matter, though. Ren was at home worrying. I knew I had a duty to get there anyway I could. My arms might be sore for a few days, but they would heal. I had to try. "It doesn't matter. My wife is waiting. She's pregnant."

"Pregnant? Right on, brother. Congrats. I guess 'Jurassic Park' was right: Life finds a way. Nice to know the human race is continuing against all odds."

"Thanks. Now you understand why I need to get there."

"I get it, man. I do." Chet chewed on his lower lip for a moment. "I think I might be able to help you, but I'm not going back out there until morning. The feral dog packs are bad around here. They tend to be more active at night. In the morning, I'll get you situated properly."

"Thanks. I appreciate it."

"Like I said, though—until then, *me casa es su casa*, brother. I'll let you bed down here for the night. In the morning, we can change those bandages, get you some new pants, and I'll see about getting you on your way."

He had a point. Ren would want me to be smart about getting home. I was safe, warm, and dry for the moment. Things would be better when the sun was in the sky. "Fair enough."

"Cool, brother. You want to watch some TV, then?"

"Sure. Sounds good."

Chet's face broke into a broad smile. "Outstanding, man."

He held out his arm for me to pull myself to a standing position again. He walked me to a large den where he had a full home theater system set up, seventy-inch flat screen, Blu-ray, surround sound—the works. Chet led me to a wall-sized rack full of DVDs of all sorts of entertainment options. "Dealer's choice, brother."

I glanced through the selection. I found a complete collection of 'Blackadder' DVDs. I plucked them from the rack and held them out for Chet. "Here, Baldrick."

Chet lit up like Christmas. "*Excellent* choice, my brother. Absolutely excellent." He clapped me on the shoulder. "You and me, we're gonna be friends. I can tell."

Chet helped me settle on the couch. He made us some cheeseless pizza, nachos with a jar of goopy cheese-like processed sauce, and brought in cold Cokes from his fridge. We spent the next couple of hours watching the riotous adventures of Sir Edmund Blackadder and his dimwitted manservant, Baldrick. He laughed. We talked. It was a legitimate good time.

Despite my constant worry for Ren and the baby, I hated to admit that it was actually fun to hang out with a guy again. It reminded me of hanging out with my friends in high school. We shot the breeze about British comedies, sci-fi, survival stuff, and life in general. I probably would have been friends with Chet before the Flu, if we had known each other. We had a lot of shared interests and similar senses of humor. He was much more gregarious than I was, though. I envied that about him.

Eventually, we both passed out on the couch. A long day had finally come to an end. I would go home after a good night's sleep.

CHAPTER THIRTEEN

The Guardian

I made myself to clean up the storm damage. It probably was not a smart thing to do, given how pregnant I was, but I reminded myself of those women throughout history who worked until the moment of giving birth. Just because I was currently housing a dependent parasite was no excuse for me to slack. I told myself that I was doing it to be responsible, that the farm depended on me. But mostly, I was doing it to keep myself busy. If I was busy, I did not have time to worry. If I did not worry, the baby seemed to be placated, and he rested comfortably.

It was difficult work, though. After the first twenty minutes, I realized that my days of squatting and bending over were coming to a close until after the kid was born. My lower back hurt. My feet were swelling. My knees were killing me. My calves hurt and the veins at the back of my knees were starting to puff out like an old lady's. I started using more tools like rakes and shovels to pick up debris and clear it from the yard. What I could burn, I burned. What couldn't burn, I moved into a pile to fix later. The missing door to the barn would have to wait until Twist got home, or

I was no longer pregnant, whichever came first. My makeshift fence boards would have to hold out until then.

I forced myself to stop and eat around midday. I built up the fire in the center of the yard. I heated a large pot of water to kill any possible bacteria left over from the filtration system, and covered it to let it cool away from the fire.

After lunch, the day became unbearably hot, one of those early autumn days when it felt more like mid-summer than fall. It was too hot to work. Just trying to move around the yard was making me pour sweat from every inch of my body and was making me dizzy. I retreated into the house to enjoy shade and the breeze from a box fan. I cranked that thing to high and sat in front of it to let it cool the sweat prickling on my forehead and chest. After a while, though, the fan suddenly died. A quick check of a nearby light told me that the house did not have enough power to run anything electric. The damage to the solar panels must have been more extensive than I thought. I had exhausted everything the batteries had stored, and the house was back to being devoid of power.

Twist had done all the solar work himself. He had read books and magazines, figured out how to wire the panels together, to run them to an inverter for the house, to wire the inverter into the house's grid, and then make a battery supply for backup. How he did it was something I could not fathom. The man was very smart. He tried to tell me that it had nothing to do with smarts. He claimed that he was only following directions, and that the people who invented all this stuff were the real geniuses. That might be true, but I know that I would never have thought to figure out how to make solar panels power a house's electrical grid. I would have just accepted a future without electricity and worked around that. I wondered if I would be able to make the solar panels work again if Twist never returned.

…if Twist never…

I hated thinking like that. He was only a day late, and suddenly he was dead to me. How morbid was I? It also made me angry that I felt so dependent on him. I used to be one of those women who wore the "A Woman Without a Man is Like a Fish Without a Bicycle" t-shirts. I was an ardent feminist. I enjoyed the company of men, but I did not need to be married. I did not need a man in my life. I was strong and independent. After the Flu, after my sister died, I was alone. I was alone, and I was surviving. I proved I was strong and independent. Then, the Last Man on Earth showed up with his proverbial White Charger of an RV, and he escorted me to the magical kingdom of Lake Houston. In the year that Twist and I have been together, I have taken advantage of him. I know it. I think he knows it, but he's too good of a man to care. I used him to get free of New York. I have depended on him for food and shelter. I convinced myself that we had a partnership, but I think he has done most of the heavy lifting, and I have let him. Could I go back to being alone and independent? Could I raise a baby in this world without him? If he never came back, would I have a choice? I remembered how emotional I got that morning after I told him I was pregnant and for that split-second I thought he'd abandoned me. I was ready to tackle the world head-on alone. And I would have. I had to get back to that sort of alpha-female tigress-mentality. Things happened. People died. It did not mean the world stopped. If Twist was dead, the sun would still rise tomorrow. This baby would need a mother. Life went on. Nothing had taught me that lesson more than the Flu. Nothing stopped when everyone died. The sun still rose. The sun still set. The seasons changed. The world kept turning. I needed to stop worrying about the *What If…* and concentrate on the *What Is*.

I gave myself a proverbial kick in the rear. Get up. Get moving. The farm is one of those *What Is*. It existed. It was real. It was present. It was a never-ending chore. It needed me at that moment. Twist or no Twist, baby or no baby, the farm existed at that moment. It would exist that night, and the next morning, too. The animals needed me. The garden needed me. I needed them. End of story. There was work to do. I put my hair up to keep it off my neck. I got a pair of leather work gloves out of the hall closet. I hitched up my maternity jeans, put on a comfy t-shirt that was two sizes too large for me. I laced up my hiking boots over my swollen feet and got to it.

The late afternoon sun was less brutal than the early afternoon sun, but the heat was still miserable. I could get some work done without sweating myself to death, at least. I kept a tall bottle of water near me at all times, and when it was empty, I refilled it from the clean water supply.

I went back to work in the garden. Fresh food, while not a pressing *need* at the moment, given our colossal stores of canned goods, was definitely a *want*. It would eventually be a very important need, but for now, we were still learning how to be farmers. I know that Twist had been reading about how to plant certain things, and when to plant them. I know he said something about rotating plants in areas because some of them used up all the particular minerals in the soil, and how other plants would return some of those minerals. We used cow manure *(of which we had a plentiful supply thanks to the Thing sisters)* as fertilizer. We mixed it into the soil when we tilled, and it seemed to work well. We also had our own compost, but that was still breaking down in the composting piles we started on the far edge of the property line, as far from the house as we could make it without making it too great a chore to get to it.

When my mom planted stuff in window boxes or pots in Brooklyn, it was simple: get a few seeds from the hardware store, drop them in some potting soil, put it in the sun, water it occasionally, and a few months later we had herbs or tomatoes. Simple. Now, the seeds were still in the hardware stores, but I had no idea if two years in the dark had harmed them. Twist said they were still good, so we planted a field of various veggies and berry plants. We planted rows of apple trees, avocado trees, peach trees, and orange trees. It would be years before they would bear fruit, and they would only be able to do that if we could keep the deer, rabbits, and other critters from munching them to nothingness before they had a chance to get started. We planted asparagus *(yuck)*, spinach *(good in salad, but otherwise, not my favorite)*, cabbage and lettuce, and blueberries, blackberries, and strawberries *(yum)*. But, it wasn't enough to have one or two of any of these plants. In order for the berry plants to bear fruit, they had to be cross-pollinated. That meant you needed *a lot* of those particular plants. And then you had to hope that bees and other bugs found those plants interesting enough to crawl around in, and then take their pollen to other plants.

The plants had to be watered a lot because Texas can be very dry in the late summer. The plants had to get enough sun, but some needed shade. Cucumbers can actually get sunburned. Who knew? Weeds outgrew the plants we actually wanted to keep at an alarming rate, so they had to be culled almost daily. You don't want weeds competing for water, sun, and minerals with your more delicate food-bearing plants. We could not guard the garden around the clock, so we had to put up waist-high fencing to try to keep the varmints out. The rabbits could dig under fencing, though. The mice, voles, and shrews could easily fit through the gaps. The deer could jump over the fence if they really wanted to get to the growing goodies beyond. Luckily, the abundance of plant life across the plains kept some of the critters from antagonizing the garden, but it was still a game where the odds were stacked against us. We were learning by doing, but it might still be a long time before we were accomplished enough to feel secure in our food acquisition abilities. And the truly annoying thing about gardening and farming is that you never "win." It never ends. Congratulations, you survived a couple of lean months in the winter. Now get back out there and do it all over again.

Some days, I was amazed that human beings had been able to live as long as they had. It felt like the balance between Life and Death was definitely slanted in Death's favor. It felt like everything in the world was trying to kill us either directly or indirectly, and we were just thumbing our noses at the long odds against us every day we chose to get out of bed. Every single day was just another day where we had to battle Fate. That might be the best metaphor for humanity that I can come up with: we're too stubborn to just die. We have the tenacity of a cockroach.

I struggled to right the wrongs the storm perpetrated on the farm. I used wooden Popsicle sticks and twine to repair and support broken stems, I clipped leaves that were too battered to self-repair, and I cleaned the debris from the garden. I kept myself so busy that I didn't think about time passing, or the lack of Twist, or the missing cow and pigs. I wasn't completely absorbed in my chores, though. Having seen a fully-grown lion up close and knowing it was still roaming around, you couldn't afford to be oblivious to that fact. I entered a strange hyper-alert state where I did not notice things like time or weather, but I flinched at every movement I spotted out of my peripheral gaze, and I heard every noise around me. I constantly looked over my shoulder to make sure nothing was sneaking up on me. When I finally thought to look up from my work, I realized it was near dusk. The sun was low in the western sky, a great orange ball touching the horizon.

I stopped working and straightened up. The muscles in my lower back, stretched out of whack from the watermelon-sized lump in my abdomen, felt like a pair of bungee cords about to snap. The back of my legs were sore, too. There was nothing I could do about that. I needed to go back to doing yoga. Working out was the first thing I quit doing after the Flu. No reason to go to the gym when there was no one to impress. Besides, scavenging for food and clean water was enough of a workout, and the added side benefit of having to ration your food was washboard abs. Remember: abs are made in the gym, but revealed while you slowly starved to death after everyone else on the planet died in a viral apocalypse.

A strange noise floated over the din of bugs and breeze, a weird, repetitive dirge, long and low. I glanced toward the barn and saw Thing 1 dancing at the door. The noise was clearly triggering her. When I saw Thing 1 in the barn, I somehow knew the noise was being made by Thing 2. Once I figured out a cow was making the noise, it made perfect sense. It was a long, miserable lowing of a scared or confused animal, maybe even one that was injured.

I sighed. I would have to go after her, no matter how much my legs and back wanted to disagree. It was the responsible thing to do. I walked back to the house, grabbed a backpack with two water bottles, my pistol, extra ammo, and a halter and lead rope. I also grabbed a walking stick because I would need the extra support.

When I walked the edges of the property around the farm, I fell more in love with Texas as a state. Living in New York, the only real images of Texas I saw were always in Westerns. Everything was flat, empty, dusty plains to me, a stray barn and windmill here and there. In actuality, the east Texas plains, while still fairly flat, were grassy with plenty of trees. Twist said it didn't look too different from some parts of Wisconsin. That wasn't a helpful reference to me, but I took it to mean that it looked like it was supposed to, and TV had lied to me.

There were plenty of gentle rolling hills around our plot of land. There were a lot of empty houses, too. Most of the houses were still waiting to be scavenged. It would be months, if not years of work to get to all of them. I enjoyed strolling the hills, even with the threat of apex predators roaming through the valleys. In New York, there's no such thing as taking a lonely stroll. There are *always* people around you. You are never alone, no matter how much you try to be. After the Flu, I got to be truly alone for the first time in my life. No sister in the next room, no mom in the kitchen downstairs, no Mrs. Escobar in the row house next door watching telenovelas all day at full volume because she's too stubborn to admit she's going deaf. At first, I hated it. I was scared all the time. I hid in my crappy, dirty little flat that I secured for myself. As time went on, and I adjusted to the pressing silence, I grew to enjoy the solitude to a degree. I didn't *love* being alone, but it was a nice change of pace.

On the farm, under that broad Texas sky, not only did I feel alone, but I felt insignificant. I gained a real sense of exactly how tiny and useless I was in the universe, especially on the nights when Twist and I took a blanket to the little hill behind the barn and looked at the stars. We were nothing but cosmic dust in the grand scheme of things, as forgettable as a mote of dust in a sunbeam. Whenever I walked around the property, or went scavenging in nearby houses, I was reminded of that fact. No matter how important we thought we were as people before the Flu, we were going back to being nothing at some point. That was an inarguable point. We would all be dust eventually. It was humbling. And frustrating. And sad.

I walked through the hills and grass toward the sound of the lowing cow. As miserable as the sound of her cries were, as long as she was making that noise, she was alive. That was enough to keep me going.

The baby fidgeted in my tummy, a reminder that I hadn't eaten dinner, yet. I slugged some water in a weak attempt to appease His Royal Highness, but I knew that wouldn't work for long. I needed to get the cow and get back.

I hiked through a small grove of trees. The cow was getting louder. When I broke through the edge of the grove into another field, I saw her. Thing 2 was standing in what used to be someone's backyard, her head stuck in the triangle made by the legs and cross-bar of a child's swing set. How she got stuck there, I have no idea.

More interesting than that, when I stumbled through the edge of the trees and saw her, I felt almost like a parent walking in on their child fooling around with a boyfriend. A large gray bull was in the middle of mounting poor, stuck Thing 2.

"Well, well, well...you little hussy." I couldn't help but smile. Is it weird that I was proud of her, to some degree? Probably. I know that's a weird thing to be proud of, but she was like my pet, almost family. No, she was family. And I was able to witness an important milestone in her life. Granted, it's a sort of strange milestone to witness, but there I was. *Today, my girl...you become a woman.*

I stood in the shade of the trees and let the bull finish having his way with my heifer. It didn't take long. As someone from the city who has never seen anything mating beyond cats, rats, and dogs, it was quite an eye-opening experience. I won't go into detail on it, but...wow. When he finished, the bull dropped off the back of Thing 2 and wandered away to graze.

I stole up to my cow, who had resumed her lowing, and helped her angle her head out of the tiny hole where she had gotten it stuck. I slipped the halter over her broad head and fastened the buckle. I patted her neck. She looked no worse for wear. "C'mon, babe. Let's go home."

Thing 2 tucked her head low and pressed into my chest. She seemed grateful to see me again. I'm sure she was confused and scared. I would have been, if I was her. It had been a big day for her.

I started strolling back to the farm, and Thing 2 followed me willingly like a large dog. She seemed to know she was going back someplace safe. I couldn't blame her. I wanted to be someplace safe, myself.

We walked halfway home when my hyper-alert senses cued me to movement in the tall grass far to the left. I stopped walking and focused on where I'd last seen something move. I squinted into the setting sun. I couldn't make anything out in the shadows of the hill below the sun. I could barely make out anything. The sun was still bright enough to blind me. I started to walk again, but froze after a thought occurred to me. Something from one of the stupid magazines Twist was always reading. He would point out articles in them. Sometimes I read them. Sometimes I just looked at the pictures. This one, though—I had glanced at it. It said something about how big cats on the African plains would often attack at dusk from the west because the setting sun would obscure them from their prey and let them sneak up on them more effectively. The moment I remembered that, I broke out into a cold sweat. Was I being stalked by a big cat?

After the Flu, I learned to trust my gut. If my "Spidey-Sense" was tingling, I had to believe something was off-kilter somewhere. I crouched low next to Thing 2 and shielded my eyes, trying to block the sun enough to get a better view into the shadows on the east side of the hills. All the grass was at least waist high. A big cat would make a lot of grass ripple if it was moving through it, but if it was crouched and waiting, it could nearly disappear. I had the ice-cold sensation that I was being watched at that very moment, and I could not tell from where. *Danger, Will Robinson.*

I held my breath and listened. Wind and crickets. I saw Thing 2 twist her head to the west, ears going into alert mode. She felt it, too. I tried to follow her gaze, but her big, dark eyes seemed to focus on the whole field at once. She turned her body so that she was facing west. I could sense anxiety from her. She was taut, ready to run. I could not even see the house or barn from where we were. The nearest shelter was a small, dark ranch-style house about three hundred yards north of us. I could hide the cow in the garage there. I could take shelter in the house. Eventually, whatever was tracking us, probably the lion, would move on. It was not the best of plans, but it was all I had at the moment. I just needed to keep an eye on the fields to the west.

I gripped my pistol hard in my right hand and started walking with the lead rope in my left. Thing 2 did not want to turn her side to the field where the big cat was hiding, but she reluctantly did at my urging. I think she trusted me to protect her. I hoped I was up to the task. I kept my trigger finger outside the trigger guard, but ready to slide into it at the first sign of trouble. I thumbed the safety button compulsively, as if I wanted to make sure it somehow did not just pop back to render my gun useless the second I needed it. I kept my eyes on the field to the left, squinting into the setting sun. I was getting spot-blind. The sun would leave large, dark afterimages in my sight, and those would blot out large swathes of the field. If I was a predatory animal, that is exactly what I would want to happen to my prey. Spot-blinded animals would never notice a big cat prowling right in front of them. My heart started to race, and my mouth became dry. I did not dare go for the water in my bag. *Focus.*

Thing 2 started to dance sideways, wanting to move farther away from the field. I caught the scent of something thick and musky on the wind, like old yeast, dried urine, and blood. It had to be the lion. For a second, I wished that Thing 2 was a horse so I could just climb on her back and ride her. I felt like I was slowing the poor cow down, that she might have a chance to outrun the lion if I wasn't slowing her down. If she wanted to bolt, there was no way I could hold onto the rope to stop her. It would strip out of my hands and give me the worst rope-burn of my life. She was an eight-hundred-and-fifty pound animal. I was going to lose that tug-of-war every day of the week.

I tried to not to keep my pace slow and even, because I knew that cats are excited by faster motion. If they think their prey is bolting, they might burst out of hiding to try to take their prey down, lest they don't get a meal that day. This cat was probably a former zoo cat, though. It was likely born in captivity. It was socialized to humans, to some degree. It had been fed by humans its whole life, but only in this post-Flu world did it have to learn to be a real lion and hunt. Did it see me as a food source? If so, would it attack me, or would it see what was around me as a food source? Either way, I did not particularly want to find out. It was probably the same lion I had shot earlier. Was it angry at me for hurting it? Did it want to seek revenge?

I had zero desire to kill this lion, oddly enough. I was prepared to do it, if I had to, but I did not *want* to see it dead. It was not the lion's fault it ate our pig. It was not the lion's fault it was feeding on caged animals. It saw easy meals. Humans are the same way. Why make food when McDonald's is easier? Microwavable meals, fast-food, pre-packaged goods—that's how we lived. Why? Because it was simple and required very little planning. This lion probably lacked a lot of the necessary hunting skills a big cat would have acquired in the wild. It was moving purely on instinct, probably scavenging rotting corpses more often than not. It was not the lion's fault it was trying to act like a lion. In a lot of ways, I felt badly for it. That cat, like some many of us, was just trying to play the bad hand he got dealt the best he could.

Everything that came next happened in an instant. I was spot-blind and squinting into the sun, a half-ton animal on a rope in one hand, a gun in the other, and the lion exploded out of its hiding spot on the grassy slope like a missile.

I had not seen it hiding. I could not have seen it. It had been in full prowl mode, crawling low and slow. The cow reacted to the motion of the beast. Thing 2 gave a panicked bawl and yanked hard to the right, away from the lion. The sudden change in her direction caught me off-guard. The rope stripped out of my hand, burning like fire. I was thrown off-balance and fell, landing hard on my right side in the tall grass. Immediately, the baby began to protest the sudden jarring by unloading an entire soccer match worth of kicks into my internal organs. The lion, caught up by the cow's motion, ignored me for a moment. I was hidden from its view, and that might have been the saving grace of the attack. If I had not fallen, I would have been the easier prey. It might have attacked me instead of Thing 2. Instead, it sprinted past me, mere feet from where I lay.

I was able to get to my knees in time to see four hundred pounds of golden African lion leap to the back of my poor little cow. The cat moved like a machine, quickly catching the much slower and more awkward cow and pouncing. Its claws sank into the cow's side, trying to find purchase to help it hold on long enough to let it attack the neck and administer a killing blow. Thing 2 bawled loudly and collapsed under the attack. Cow and lion rolled through the grass. The cow's weight rolling over the cat made the lion relinquish its claw attack momentarily. Thing 2 rolled back to her feet and tried to run. I could see the dark red slashes in her flesh bleeding freely. The cat tried to rush her again.

I wasted no time in sighting down the barrel of my gun and popping off four quick shots. The bullets hit the cat broadside. At a range of maybe fifteen yards, each bullet found a home in the cat's muscled body. The bullets were small-caliber, though. They stung the cat. They were a painful bite, wounding shots, but they were not killing shots, not through the thick hide and muscle walls. I needed to hit it someplace vital.

The bullets were enough to make the cat reevaluate its targets, though. The cow could be easily caught again. I was the true threat, though. The cat wheeled on me. There was only a little distance between us. At full speed, the cat could close that gap in a heartbeat. It sprang at me, maw gaping and snarling viciously. The cat's snarl reverberated through my chest. I felt my heart seize. My pulse was hammering in my temples. A heavy drape of pure fear fell across my shoulders and my hands started to tremble. I did the only thing I could do and started squeezing the trigger as hard and as fast as I could.

The lion's broad face made a good target. I saw blood and flesh spray from the animal's head as the bullets landed. It had so much weight and momentum behind it, I could not stop it in time. It was a freight train. It slammed hard into me. I managed to twist my body to right, taking the full brunt of impact on my left shoulder and upper back. The force of the animal hitting me sent me flying, though. I remember the gun leaving my hand. I simply couldn't hold onto it. It disappeared into the grasses, never to be found again. I remember being airborne for a split second, tumbling through the air with only one thought on my mind: Protect the baby. I wrapped my arms around my stomach and tried to get a foot under me to twist myself around so I could take the landing flat on my back. Somehow, through a miracle or profoundly innate protective instinct, I managed to keep my bulging belly from handling any of the fall. As I planted my right leg, I felt something pop in my knee. I managed to turn and take the full landing on my back and neck. All the air was knocked out of me. I couldn't breathe. I couldn't figure out how to breathe, either. I slapped the ground around me with one hand, trying to find the gun. I expected the lion to come around any second to finish me off. I could hear it near me in the grass. I could hear snuffling and heavy, labored breaths. The Mama Bear in me was trying to fight through the pain and the panic. I couldn't though. I just couldn't. I felt a hard wave of pain rip through my abdomen. I couldn't even breathe through the pain. I started to see spots.

Relax, Ren. Somehow, I heard my father's voice in the back of my head. *Relax. You aren't going to die.* It was a memory from when I was a kid. He had been trying to teach me to catch a baseball. I mishandled a throw, taking it off the heel of my glove. The ball had popped up and hit me square in the throat. I couldn't get my breath. Everything hurt. Like any kid would, I went into full drama queen mode. Grunting screams, panic, tears—the works. My father, with his big, calloused, working man's hands, held me in his arms. *Relax,* he'd said. Something about his voice calmed me. I stopped freaking out, the pain ebbed away, and I got to my feet. It was another year before I dared try to catch a baseball again, but I lived. My dad was right. *Relax.* I started to repeat my manta. *You will be fine. You will be fine. You will be fine.*

Suddenly, I could breathe again. My lungs figured out how to inhale. The dark spots in my vision cleared. I hissed a heavy, cleansing breath through my teeth. I pushed myself to an awkward sitting position, cradling my belly with my right arm. The baby was thrashing. *Easy, kiddo.*

I struggled to my feet, desperately looking for my gun, or any weapon actually. I found a fist-sized rock in the weeds, but that was it. It was better than nothing. I raised the rock, ready to thump it off the charging lion's nose, but I saw the lion wasn't charging. There was a large mound of big cat lying in the grass ten feet away. It was no longer breathing. I moved around it and saw that one of my shots had punctured its skull, almost nearly right between the eyes. The poor lion was dead.

I let the rock fall out of my hand. I looked for Thing 2. She was standing placidly nearby, the slashes in her back staining the white patches of fur on her sides bright red. She seemed to understand that the lion was no longer a threat.

I stood on wavering legs. My right knee hurt fiercely. I had twisted it, or sprained it, or even popped a ligament somewhere. I could stand, but it hurt to put weight on my leg. What if I'd blown my ACL? It wasn't like I could get surgery to fix that. *Deal with one problem at a time, Ren.*

I limped toward the cow. She let me gather the lead rope. The palm of my hand had a wicked red welt from where the rope had burned me when she'd yanked away. The skin was gone leaving a strip of glossy, red, bleeding flesh. *Ignore the pain, Ren.*

I grabbed the rope, and started to walk back toward the barn. It was still a long way away. It was going to be long, painful struggle back to barn. I leaned on the cow, using her like a makeshift crutch. When I could, kept my right leg bent, crow-hopping with the cow as my support. It was a slow walk back to the barn, but through sheer grit and determination, and the help of my pretty Thing 2, I somehow made it.

Thing 2 walked straight to the rear door of the barn. She knew what lay beyond. I opened the door for her, and she stormed through it, running to Thing 1, and nuzzling her sister for support. I knew I needed to clean her wounds, possibly get some stitches in them, but that was going to have to wait. At that moment, I just could not do another thing.

As I stood in the doorway of the barn in the fading light of the day, I was doubled-over by a rippling wave of pain low in my guts. It was like my body was involuntarily clenching every muscle in my stomach. It was an unmistakable, terrifying pain.

I was having a contraction.

CHAPTER FOURTEEN

Home is Where the Heart Is

I was startled awake to find a big, smiling, bearded face almost directly over my own face. "Hey, bud! Time to rise and shine! We gotta get that bandage changed."

Chet whistled a cheery tune as he peeled the bandage from my hip. It was crusty with dried blood, and when he peeled it away, it pulled at the scabbed areas of the wound and caused them to bleed afresh. He appraised it with a smile. "It don't look too bad. That's a good thing."

It did not look too bad, he was correct in that assumption. However, it looked bad enough. The entry point of the slug was still open and bleeding. The area around it was mottled and stained with blood and bruising. The left side of my hip and lower abdomen was a deep shade of purple from the trauma of the blast. It would be for several weeks. Something that like was a slow heal.

"Doesn't look like infection is setting in yet, but it is probably too early to tell." Chet handed me a bottle of capsules. "Take three of these a day, morning, noon, and evening. They'll help stave off infection."

I took the pills from him. "Thanks, Chet. I really have to get home now. You said you had a plan."

Chet crossed his arms in front of him like a genie. "What Master wishes, Master gets." He gave an exaggerated Barbara Eden-style blink. "It's down the street. C'mon."

Chet helped me limp down the street. He told me he had a plan to get me back to the farm, come hell or high water. In the garage of a neighbor's house, he pulled open the door to reveal a golf cart. Chet thumped the plastic roof of the cart proudly. "My neighbor was a big golfer. This here cart is street-legal. Top speed around thirty miles an hour. This will get you home."

"It will go thirty miles?"

Chet shrugged. "Should. Look at the battery pack in it." He lifted the hood of the little cart. A large array of car batteries powered it. "We are just going to have to charge the batteries, first. We can do that at the house. Shouldn't take too long. Four hours, tops."

I did the mental calculations. Five, maybe six hours before I would get home. It was better than walking. And it wasn't like I had another choice. "Let's do it."

Chet put the cart into neutral and pushed it down the street. I crutched along behind him.

"So, this wife of yours—what's she like?"

"She's great. The best."

"You marry her before the Flu, or after?"

I told him the story of how I met Ren, and how she saved me from bleeding out after a tiger attacked me, and how we were building a farm near a lake. I held back the location, though. Like Chet said the night before, it was hard to know who to trust. Part of me wanted to invite him out there. He could help us farm. We could put him in the house down the street so we could all still have our privacy. I knew he was set up well in Houston, though. It would be silly for him to abandon a house with so many conveniences to come try to rebuild at Lake Houston.

I decided to broach the subject of farming with him as we

walked back into his driveway. "How long do you figure you can last without planting crops?"

Chet was digging an electrical cord out of a pile of stuff in his garage. He plugged one end into a wall socket, and hooked the other end to the charging plug at the front of the cart. He put his hands on his hips and looked around at the neighborhood around us. "I guess I never really thought about it. I had a year's worth of stuff ready to go before the Flu. After everyone died, I scavenged a bunch of stuff from the neighbor's houses and the nearby stores. I probably have three or four years of canned goods and boxed non-perishables. So, probably three or four more years."

"You're going to have to farm eventually."

"Probably." Chet did not seem fazed by the prospect of having to farm. "I figured I'd jump off that bridge when I came to it. A lot can happen in three years. Might be I die of a heart attack before then. Or maybe I get shot by one of the psychos roaming Houston. Who can predict the future, am I right?"

"You did a pretty good job of predicting the future when it came to preparing for the Flu."

Chet shrugged one shoulder and waved off my compliment. "Got lucky, is all. I saw some data and took a risky gamble on it. It could have worked out pretty poorly for me."

I decided I'd invite him out to the farm, without actually inviting him. "Listen, man—I'll be back on the north side here a few more times, I'm sure. I'll stop back in and check on you, provided you promise not to shoot me again."

"Just knock on the front door and shout your name, brother. I promise I'll put the gun down before answering." He laughed. "I'd appreciate you checking on me, though. Nice to know there are good people out there."

"Maybe someday you can move out to the farm with me and Ren. There are a lot of houses around our place. You can take one of them."

Chet looked embarrassed. He kicked at the concrete floor of his garage with the toe of his sneaker. "I dunno, man. This is my house. It's where I've lived for the last fifteen years. I'm not really inclined to just bail on it. Plus, I've got all my stuff…"

I held up my hand. "I get it. I do." It had been hard to leave a lot of my old stuff back in Wisconsin. "It's an offer on the table for the future, is all. Come out, don't come out. You do what makes you comfortable."

"I appreciate the offer, though. You got a standing offer for a place to sleep any time you show up here, though. We can watch movies and stuff. Always glad for the company. Bring the wife and that baby when it comes."

"Maybe I will." The words hung in the air between us. It felt like we had already said our good-byes, and there was only awkward silence left. It was uncomfortable.

"Well, hell. This is gonna take a while. You want to watch some 'Star Trek' or something?" Chet scratched behind his ear.

I nodded. "Make it so, Number One."

The cart started easily after five hours on the charger. We watched six episodes of 'Star Trek: The Next Generation' in that time, and had a simple lunch of canned tuna and Triscuits. Chet loaded me up with some more bandages and salves. "Just in case, man." He also gave me a few bottles of water and some snacks. He put the crutches in the bag-holding racks on the rear of the cart.

Chet and I shook hands after I positioned myself behind the wheel of the cart. "Remember the way back," he said. "Be glad to see you again, anytime."

"I will," I promised. "I'll look for a ham radio out there. Probably got to be another one somewhere. Maybe you'll hear from me before too long."

"I'd like that. I'll look for one, too. Maybe next time you show up, I'll have one for you."

There wasn't anything else to say. I double-checked my shotgun, making sure it was loaded and the safety was on. I rested it on the seat next to me, keeping it in easy reach. I shifted the cart to reverse and stepped on the pedal. The cart's electric motor whirred to life, and I rolled down the driveway and bounced over the lip of the street. I felt a jolt of pain ripple through my hip. The seat springs were bouncy and absorbed some of the rough road, but it was going to be a long trip home, regardless.

I shifted to Drive, and the little cart spun its tires for a second, caught the pavement, and launched me forward. It got to speed quickly, and I was on my way.

Right away, I started feeling lighter, as if a great weight was being lifted from my shoulders. It was only the early afternoon, and I was heading back to Ren. I would be there in an hour, maybe a little longer. For the first time since I left the house two days ago, I felt good. I had wasted the trip by having to abandon everything I'd come for, but I could always get those supplies again. I'd lost Hera, but someday I could get another horse. I'd been shot, but like Chet had assured me repeatedly, I'd live. I'd learned some possible truths about the Flu. I'd learned that there were a number of people gathering in the major cities. I'd learned that civilization might return someday in the distant future. All things considered, this trip could have gone much worse for me. I was desperate to get home to put Ren's mind at ease. I wanted to hold her again. I wanted to see my farm again.

The first thirty minutes of the drive went well. I twisted through the suburbs and found Highway 69 North, the road that would take me most of the way back to Lake Houston. On the empty highway, I enjoyed the breeze the cart generated through the open sides. It was not the most conventional of vehicles, but it was a welcome ride, regardless.

I saw a lot of animals on the way home. In the suburbs, I saw a large pack of dogs. The feral packs had learned quickly to revert to the "wolf" part of their brains to stay alive. The packs were growing quickly, expanding with new additions and puppies. I knew that they would probably become a problem in the future. Nothing made me feel sicker than the thought of having to hunt dogs to keep their numbers under control, but I could already see that day coming. I saw a pair of rhinoceroses wading through a field of corn, eating their body weight of the towering stalks. At one point, a mixed group of kangaroos and antelope bounded across the highway in front of me. It was a strange sight to see the two very different animals merging as a single mob and bounding along together in a similar fashion. There were herds of cattle moving as a single group. There were deer herds, no doubt the future prey of those feral dogs as they moved closer to their lupine ancestors. I saw flocks of turkey, geese, and ducks. The whole world north of the city seemed to be completely stocked with game. In that game, I saw my future, and my baby's future. The game, the garden, the solar panels—we were on the correct path to living a beautiful future. I could not wait for that future.

It struck me then that I was actually excited for what would be in the future, instead of mourning what was in the past. My vision was set firmly on what was coming next instead of being consumed by the present. It had taken a long time to put the past behind me, to move past the deaths of all my family and friends, but I had somehow done it. I had waded through a river of misery and suffering, and I'd come out clean on the other side. I had made a new family to fill the void of the family I'd lost. I'd just made a new friend. I was living *for* something instead of just living. For the first time since the first kid in my old high school died of the Flu, I was actually happy and excited. It felt strange. It was a good strange, but definitely strange. Two years of putting on the brave face, two years of struggle, two years of uncertainty, and it was finally feeling like it was all over. I had adjusted to life as it was, and I was embracing it fully. Of course, karma conspired to kick me in the butt the second I started to get happy again.

The engine in the cart died suddenly. The high-pitched electric whir cut out to silence. The cart rolled to a stop in the space of twenty yards. No amount of curses or hope could start it again. The batteries had given their all. I was at least twelve or fifteen miles from Chet's, and probably twenty miles from the farm. There was no question which direction I would head, and there was also no question how badly it would hurt to get there.

I eased myself out of the cab of the cart, slipped into my backpack and put my shotgun over my head and shoulder to wear across my back. I put the crutches under my arms and started the long, slow process of gimping my way back to Ren.

I made good progress for the first mile and a half. I kept a decent pace, did not shift my hip too much, and felt like I could keep it up as long as I needed. Then, my forearms and armpits decided to weigh in with their learned opinion of the situation. That slowed me up considerably. I was quickly rubbed raw in a tender area beneath my arms on the inside of my biceps and the delicate flesh on the sides of my trunk. Every step, every movement became painful. I could ignore pain for a time. After another half-mile, I was chaffed to the point of agony. I had blisters forming. I reluctantly had to stop using the crutches. This forced me to put some weight on my left leg, which in turn put stress on my hip. I abandoned the crutches on the side of the road; they were dead weight to me at that point. I found a long branch under a tree in someone's yard. I used my knife to cut off the excess twigs and limbs, and I fashioned a decent walking stick to help me bear some weight. It was not the best solution, but it was something. All that mattered was that I keep going.

I made it another half-mile at a snail's pace. I had to step forward on my right leg quickly, then drag my left leg behind me, a sort of awkward hop-step. Each step caused heavy jolts of pain to pop through my hip and thigh. It was manageable pain, though. It would not stop me. I told myself that it was just a serious bruise. You can get through a serious bruise. It's painful, sure; it won't kill you, though. It just hurts, is all. I remember my wrestling coach talking about the difference between *hurt* and *injured*. You could wrestle if you were hurt; injury was put you on the bench. Just grit your teeth and keep grinding.

I started to sweat profusely. It was a brutally hot fall day. Texas seemed to be rife with unbearably hot days. I remember hearing that if you move to a warm climate, you would adapt to the climate eventually, and then I'd start thinking sixty degrees was cold, but for now, I was struggling in the heat. Sweat cascaded down my face and soaked the neck of my shirt. The sweat irritated the raw spots under my arms and on my sides. I started feeling a lot of sweat of on my left side, near the wound. That made me look down. I saw a bright red spot where fresh blood had soaked through the bandage on my hip. All the movement had caused the wound to bleed again. I had to stop and change my bandage, tossing the old gauze into a ditch and pressing a new, clean, dry bandage to the spot.

I drank some water as long as I was stopped. I had two large bottles of clean water, thanks to Chet. If I had been able to cart it all the way home, they would have been more than enough. However, with the fifteen-plus miles I'd have to drag myself, in the heat, with the amount of blood I was losing, I wondered if I would have enough water to get me there. I might have to break into some houses and search for water, and if it came to it, find a creek somewhere and risk dysentery.

I'd like to be able to say that I gritted my teeth and powered through the pain. I'd *like* to be able to say that, but the truth is that whole situation got to me and almost broke me down. I didn't cry. Not really. But, saline bubbled up on my lower eyelids like tears. They didn't spill out, but they were there. I had to swipe them away with the back of my hand. I cursed myself out for being soft. I had dealt with so much in the past two years that this situation was just icing on the cake. It was not going to make me crack. *Man up!* I thought about Ren, and the baby, and the farm. They needed me. I was going to them. Fifteen miles was not too far for me to go. It was a long walk, sure. At my current pace, I had to estimate it would take me ten or twelve hours. Maybe thirteen. Maybe more. I would not make it by dark, even with the sun out until well past nine in the evening. Might not even make it by the dawn the next morning if I walked all night. It was a trial of stamina I was determined to pass. No amount of crying, complaining, or wishing would make it any easier.

Even with the bitter sting of sweat on my wounds, I forced myself to keep walking. I tried to make it into a game, rewarding myself for completing little challenges. I would spot a tree at the end of a long block. If I made it without stopping, I could rest for three minutes in the shade of that tree. If I had to stop, I wouldn't allow myself the relief of the shade. I tried to sing old songs I used to like that I thought I'd forgotten. If I could remember all the lyrics to Blink-182's "Adam's Song," then I could drink water while I rested. If not, I would have to power though without a drink for another quarter-mile. Anything I could do to keep myself moving, focused, and directed, I did.

A mile slipped by. Then another one. And another. I watched the sun fall in the west, dropping behind the peaked roofs of a mid-90s subdivision. Once the sun stopped providing direct rays of heat on my back, I started to feel a chill. The breeze out of the northwest picked up as the temperature shifted. The sweat that had soaked my shirt and jeans was now drying icy-cold on my body and making my teeth chatter. I shivered. I was from Wisconsin. I *knew* shivering. Something was wrong. This was an altogether different sensation from shivering because of cold. I felt weird. Queasy. Light-headed. When I stopped to change my hip bandage again, I realized that the skin around the wound was red, swollen, and hot to the touch. It hurt when I applied pressure. The wound was becoming infected despite my best efforts to prevent it. I had taken three of the pills Chet had given me, but they did not seem to be working properly. Maybe they were inert? Maybe I resistant to them? Who knew?

I busted the door handle on the nearest house, a nice, ranch-style, and forced the door open. A wave of dry, distilled death smell smacked me in the face. I apologized to the two mummified corpses in the living room for intruding, what looked like a father and daughter. With my Maglight illuminating the way, I found the master bathroom of the house. A third dried corpse was splayed haphazardly across the queen-sized bed in the master bedroom. The mother.

I searched the cupboards and drawers of the dual-sink vanity in the bathroom. I found dozens of brown pill bottles with white caps, and large bottles of hydrogen peroxide and rubbing alcohol. Chet had given me amoxicillin. I found a bottle of tetracycline in one of the mother's drawers. I popped the top and swallowed three pills. I knew enough about medicine at this point to know they were two different types of antibiotics, prescribed for different reasons, but I didn't know the reasons. I didn't know if they would react against each other or cancel each other out, or anything. I just knew the amoxicillin did not seem to be working, so I was trying something new. In the bathroom, I peeled off the blood bandage on my hip and doused the wound with hydrogen peroxide. It immediately frothed into a fountain of pink foam. I rinsed the foam from the wound with the rubbing alcohol. The sting of it made stars explode in front of my eyes, and I screamed out in pain. It was a good pain, though. It woke me up. It felt cleansing. I repeated the peroxide and alcohol rinse again, slathered Neosporin into the wound, and bandaged it again. My medical attentions were not going to win any awards, but they would keep me going for now.

The queasy feeling did not go away, though. My stomach churned like I was going over an ocean wave suddenly, and I vomited into the bathtub. The three pills I had just taken came back out rudely. I rinsed my mouth with the last of my water and spat into the tub. I put some nearly-dry toothpaste on my finger and swabbed it around my teeth. Minty.

I staggered out to the kitchen of the house and looked for water. They had a half-dozen cans of Coke in the fridge, but the cans were covered with the remnants of dried mold. I did not feel like risking a different infection.

There was nothing I could do, but move to the next house and look for water there. And then the next house after that if I came up empty. I went through four houses before I found a stash of clean water. The fourth house had a stack of Poland Spring water, all in the sixteen-ounce bottles. I tossed eight of them into my backpack and kept walking.

Night settled heavily over the landscape. I became progressively sicker as I walked. The lack of food in my stomach did nothing to help that. I tried to force myself to swallow a bit of a granola bar, but it was like eating wood and tar. It felt thick in my mouth and made the gorge rise in the back of my throat. I had nothing left in my stomach to throw up, so I dry-heaved until my ribs hurt, instead.

Another mile. And another. My pace fell off even further. I was staggering along, stabbing my walking stick into the ground and dragging myself to it, a shambling man.

When my tired legs finally gave out, I collapsed. I lay in the thick, overgrown grass of someone's lawn. The grass was brittle from sun, heat, and lack of water. It made my skin itch. I poured a bottle of water over my face and head to cool myself down. I knew I had a fever, but it felt low-grade. How much of what I was feeling was heat-related, and how much was infection-related? Hyperthermia could be fatal. So could an infection. Either way, I was not in good shape.

I had hoped to be home before dawn. Now, I knew that my body was simply not going to let me do that. I needed to rest. I needed sleep. I needed some time to recover. I hated being away from Ren, but it was physically impossible for me to continue on that night.

I wanted to get into a house, get someplace safe. My head was swimming. I tried to drag myself to my feet, clenching my teeth and trying to find that final shred of intestinal fortitude deep within my soul that would allow me to get to shelter. The well was dry, though. I had nothing left in the tank, and I collapsed in the middle of that lawn. A wave of sickness washed over me, I felt the chilling shudder of fever ripple through my neck, cheeks, and forehead, and then I passed out. It was the only thing I could do.

CHAPTER FIFTEEN

Delivery

It was too soon. The baby was coming far too soon. By my estimates, the baby should have come in very late fall. It was only early fall. It was at least a month too early. The pain was unquestionably a contraction, though. It was a full-body clenching that seemed to originate in my pelvis. I had never experienced a full contraction before, but I just *knew* what it was. Call it a Mother's Instinct. The pain of it doubled me over, and I clutched at my swollen belly.

I was in a barn. How very Biblical. I was surrounded by two cows and a few pigs, all looking at me curiously and expecting food. Not today, friends. I wished I could stay and feed all of them, but I had other, more pressing engagements.

When the contraction passed, and I could breathe again, I limped toward the house. Labor could take hours. There was no rush. Every nerve in my body was on fire, though. Anxiety and fear coursed through my veins instead of blood.

I was in a farmhouse in the middle of an empty Texas prairie. I had very few drugs and no help. I felt a wracking sob ripple out of my throat before I could stop it. I should have help. I should have been in a hospital with trained medical staff, epidurals, and emergency equipment. I should have had ice chips, ginger ale, and little plastic cups of Jell-O. My mom should have been there. My sister should have been there. My dad and my brother should have been in the waiting room nervously passing the time. Twist should be there. My jaw trembled. *Damn it, Twist. Where are you?*

I swallowed hard and forced myself to bury the fear. I reminded myself to think, yet again, of all the other women who had done this without doctors, without hospitals or medicine. *You will be fine. You will be fine. You will be fine.*

I had been preparing mentally for this moment. I had a checklist of things in my head. Get clean towels. Start boiling water. I had the birth supplies I'd looted from a hospital just after I admitted to myself that I was pregnant. I needed to methodically go about my business and —

Another contraction ripped into me. It hit so hard and fast that my breath was stolen from lungs. I groaned and grabbed at a chair in the yard for support. That second contraction had come awfully fast. How could it come that fast? What was the time on that? Three minutes? Two? I felt a hot gush run down the insides of my legs. My water had definitely broken. This baby was coming *now*. There was going to be no long labor. It was on its way, whether or not I wanted it to be.

The contraction passed. I tried to hustle to gather all necessary items. I pushed the cauldron of water over the fire in the yard to get it hot. I limped into the house and gathered the towels and birthing supplies. Another contraction hit me, but I was ready for it. I froze and let it wash over me, breathing through my teeth. The pain was extreme, indeed. It was the most pain I'd ever felt in my life. However, I could handle it. It was not made-for-television pain. It was uncomfortable. It was agonizing. It was not pleasant in the least, but I felt better about it. I had been dreading the pain for months. I had done a neonatal rotation in my nursing studies, so I had been present for births, but given that all those women had been on epidurals to manage the pain, I was highly suspect of dealing with the raw pain without drugs to manage the discomfort. Of course, the baby had not hit the birth canal yet, so maybe I was giving myself a false hope.

I decided to have the baby in the bathtub in the master bedroom. It was a large, wide tub, one of those over-sized jobs with hot tub jets and a sloped back for relaxing. Without running water in the house, we had never used it, but I used to daydream about getting it running with hot, clean water, maybe a little bubble bath for good measure, and just languishing in it. It would be a good place for delivery. I could use the wall to brace my feet, if necessary. Given my height, the tub was plenty big. And it would be easier to clean than the mattress on the bed. Maybe it was a little more bourgeoisies than Caroline Ingalls delivering Baby Carrie in a hand-built cabin on the Kansas plains, but to each her own. I was willing to bet Caroline would have traded places with me in a heartbeat.

I carried the towels and supplies to bathroom. I brought several bottles of water. I brought some snacks if I needed them, too. Granola, beef jerky, and a box of Swiss Cake Rolls I'd been saving just for this event. Fester followed me, knowing something was afoot. I could not tell if there was genuine concern in him, or if this was just because he enjoyed beef jerky, as well. He posted himself on the edge of the sink to watch whatever was going to happen, his black tail twitching lazily.

The cauldron of water was percolating pleasantly. There was no way I could carry the entire cauldron full of water to the bathroom, so I just dipped a pot into it. I stripped out of my clothes, leaving them on the patio outside the back door.

Naked, I walked back to the bathtub. I gingerly stepped

over the edge and climbed into it, gripping the sides. I took a deep, cleansing breath. I was as ready as I was ever going to be. *Bring it, kid. I'm ready for you.*

And then the real pain started.

Contractions were one thing. The abstract, overwhelming pain of a football-sized being moving through the birth canal to the waiting world was a whole 'nother ball game, son. When the real labor started not long after I took up my position in the tub, I knew that I was in a world of trouble.

—As an aside, can I rant for a second about a part of me being referred to as a "canal?" I'm as vain as the next girl, I guess. I try not to put too much stock in physical appearance, but I like to look nice and feel good about myself. Thinking of something inside me as a "canal" is absolutely mortifying. Anyhow…

The first *serious* contraction hit me like wildfire. It was a blinding rage of exquisite pain that almost made me wish for death. I was wholly *not* prepared for something that intense. The first dozen contractions before that one had given me false hope. I felt like I was being ripped open. I managed to get through the first wave without screaming, but when the contraction passed, I nearly passed out from joy. The manageable pain felt like a pleasant massage compared to the intensity of the contraction. I wondered if I had dilated enough to let this baby through. I tried not think about the damage that could be done to both me and the baby if I wasn't. I tried not to think about the complications. I tried not to worry about the *What Ifs*. That was easier said than done, of course. The *What Ifs* flew around in my brain like bats leaving a cave. Only when the waves of contraction pain hit me was I able to ignore them, focusing only on the intensity of what was happening to me in the moment.

I knew that I needed to resist the urge to bear down and push until I knew I was absolutely ready for it, but I had no way of really determining when that would be. I was playing this purely on instinct, the way that mothers-to-be had for centuries before modern medicine stepped in and figured out the science behind bringing another human being into the world.

During the periods between contractions, I tried to calm myself by telling myself that I was a trained nurse, even if I hadn't quite graduated when the Flu hit. I would have been an RN inside of a month. I had training. I knew what I was doing, even given the inconvenience of the baby coming out of me, and not someone else. I could handle the technical aspects of the birth, maybe not the practical aspects, but I definitely had a handle on the technical aspects. I tried to tell myself how much worse I could be having it. I was in a clean house. I had water. I had food. I had medical supplies. I was in really good shape, statistically speaking.

None of my constant pep-talk was helping me keep down my fears. The pain did, though. When the contractions hit hard, there was literally nothing I could do other than focus on the pain. It was too overwhelming to think about anything else. Each contraction was just an exercise in pain management. When the contraction would finally ebb away, I would collapse back against the cool surface of the tub, sweaty and grateful the pain stopped. I wanted ice chips. I wanted ice chips more than anything, but we had never gotten around to getting the freezer running, not that it would have helped with the solar panels and wiring damaged in the last storm. As it was, I was in the dark with only a pair of LED camping lanterns providing light. Ice was a dream for the future.

Another contract brought itself upon me. I wanted them to stop. I wanted them over. I could feel things shifting and moving in me. It was unsettling. I knew the time to actually bear down was coming. That was a terrifying prospect in itself. I wasn't ready to be a mother. I was ready to have this baby out of me, certainly. But, I did not feel *matronly*, yet. I did not feel like someone's mother. I wondered if it was that way with all mothers. Did they feel unprepared when the baby came? Did they feel like they would fail as a parent?

I could feel a contraction building. The time had come. There was no more avoiding it. I gripped the edges of the tub, leaned forward, and pushed into the pain. I strained. I felt pressure building in my head and chest. My vision wavered. And then the contraction passed, and I was able to relax for a few moments. I had no idea if the contraction did any good. I had no idea if the baby was making progress. I had to assume he was.

That's how the next hour or so progressed. Contraction. Push. Nearly pass out from the strain. Rest. Do it again. It felt like it was taking forever. I started to get scared. Was I doing it right? Was the baby in trouble? The physical and mental stresses of the process took their toll on me. After a contraction passed, I would break down in tears. I was not ready for this. I wanted Twist to be there. I wanted a doctor. I wanted someone to cut this baby out of me C-Section Style. I was too hot, and I wanted to be cool. I just wanted it to be over with. I was too tired, too sore, and too miserable to keep going. I wanted to be one of those strong women who can have a baby and then make dinner for their families, but I wasn't. I couldn't. I was done. I wanted to quit. I didn't want the baby anymore. I was a horrifying jumble of insane emotions and exhaustion.

And then suddenly, the baby was crowning. I don't know when I noticed that part of it in the process, but I reached down and felt the soft dome of a tiny head covered with fine, wet, peach fuzz hair. The baby was coming out in the proper position. It was nearly there. I exhaled a massive sigh of relief. The head was the tough part. Once the head was out, the baby usually slid out in a lump just after that. I was nearly done! I'm not sure what I was overjoyed about more: the baby's head or the prospect of being done with the whole process.

With the next contraction, I promised myself I was getting this kid out of me in the next few minutes. I knew it might take more than one contraction, but I wanted to give him everything I had. The crowning gave me a renewed vigor. I could see the proverbial light at the end of the tunnel, which is an idiom that has a particular potency in this situation.

Two more sessions of pushing, and I felt the head pop through all the way. I continued to push, reaching to grab the baby by the neck and shoulders, and suddenly—there was an entire baby in my hands.

I fell back against the slope in the tub, trembling and crying. It was not a sad crying, but tears were just leaking from my eyes. I grabbed a towel and started to clear the mucus and fluids off the baby's face. I used a suction bulb to clear the nostrils and mouth. The tiny little mouth opened, it coughed once, gasped for air, and then a healthy, angry wail sounded. The baby's high-pitched cries were like music to me. The baby was healthy, breathing, and pissed-off at the whole birth process. I understood that. We were on the same page there.

As I cleaned the tiny body, I realized quickly that my prophecy of a baby boy had been wrong. I had given birth to a little girl! I had been so certain of her being a boy, that I never even considered the possibility of delivering a girl. She was very small, though. She did not look premature, but she was definitely undersized for a healthy newborn.

I swaddled her in a towel, marveling at the tiny limbs and hands and feet. I cleared her eyes gently with the tips of my thumbs. She had bright blue eyes—probably from Twist's side. My family all had mud-brown eyes. I could see a lot of Twist in her face. I could see a lot of my mother, too.

As I relaxed with this little life in my arms, I knew I was ready to be a mother. It happened the moment I saw her. All doubt in my mind was erased. I was going to mother the hell out of this little girl, and no one was ever going to stop me from that. I knew she was hungry. Babies needed to eat shortly after birth. I moved her down to my breast, cradling her with my right arm. She latched onto the nipple easily and naturally. I relaxed in the tub, beads of sweat drying on my forehead, grateful to be done with the process.

I felt a hard twitch low in my belly. I began having another contraction. Was it the afterbirth? I reached down between my legs and felt the soft dome of another tiny head. My heart leapt to my throat. I was having twins.

CHAPTER SIXTEEN

The Last Ten Miles

When I was unconscious, I have to believe the conscious part of my brain was scrapping to come back to the light. Unconsciousness was simple. It was dark and cool and soothing. It was so good that I have no memory of it. Consciousness is a fight. It's aware and vigilant. It wants to be there, to protect and defend. Unconsciousness is a cop-out, says the conscious part of my brain. If the unconscious part of my brain had a voice, it would probably tell the conscious part of my brain to shut up, because unconsciousness is so easy. The conscious part of my brain knew that I was in danger, though. It knew that there were packs of feral dogs, wild animals, and dehydration. It knew that I was vulnerable, splayed out on someone's lawn with zero defenses. My brain knew that I needed to stay alive. Its sole job was to keep me breathing, and thus it somehow dragged me back from the abyss and forced my eyes to open.

It was still night. A field of stars was arrayed overhead, and without light pollution, it looked like I could see every speck of detail in the galaxy. That was one of the bright spots about the post-Flu world: the heavens always looked amazing now. It wasn't just the major stars that got through the atmosphere, it was all the stars, a wild, paint-splattered canvas of miniscule pinpoints of light. Trillions of fires burning in space, letting you know simultaneously that you're not alone in the universe, but yet you are.

I wanted to sit up, but everything hurt. My muscles were cramping from exertion and dehydration. The infection in my side was bad. The skin I had rubbed raw from crutching was blistered. My entire body felt like one giant raw nerve.

I heard grass crunch near my head. Something was nearby. Something big. My shotgun was still strapped across my back. I was lying on it. I couldn't get it without rolling over and getting to my knees. I craned my neck, tilting my head so I could looking behind me. I saw a large shadow near the house. Very large.

I took the chance and forced myself to roll over, grabbing the stock of the shotgun and spinning it to my hip as I did, pointing the barrel at the shadow. The sudden movement startled the animal, and I saw a head toss, and it side-stepped. Then, unafraid, it walked forward and buried a big, wide head into my chest. I felt tears well into my eyes. Hera had somehow found me. "Hello, stupid horse."

I wrapped my arms around her face. I have no idea how she found me. I do not know if horses can track like dogs, but they must have some sort of ability to find their herd after being separated. I can only imagine that she was heading back toward the farm and stumbled across my scent. Upon finding me passed out in the yard, she must have stuck around to stand watch over me.

Hera's arrival had given me my way to get back home. I couldn't walk, but I could ride. It would not be a comfortable ride, given that the saddle and bridle were still back on the cart on the side of the road, and I'm sure that straddling the horse would really hurt my hip, but it was a far better alternative to trying to limp home.

Sucking wind through my teeth as the pain lit though me, I struggled to my feet. Hera stood patiently. I grabbed some of her mane with my left hand. I knew it was going to hurt a lot, especially since I needed to launch off my left leg. I tried, but could not get enough power to swing up and onto her back. I had to walk her to a Honda Accord rotting in the street. I climbed onto the hood of the car, then threw myself onto her back bodily, like a sack of potatoes, and spun into a proper riding position.

"Let's go home, girl." I tapped my heels into her side and tugged her mane to the right, away from the car. She wheeled away from the car and started trotting. The up-and-down motion of a trot was like being set on spikes. Every bounce ricocheted pain through my body. I dropped my hips and tugged backward on her mane. She seemed to know what I wanted, because she slowed to a walk. It still hurt, but it wasn't bright, stinging, electric pain. It was a dull, manageable ache. I could deal with a minor throb. I'd had worse. At that pace, it would take at least two or three hours to get back to the farm. Judging by the night sky and the lack of gray in the east, I would probably get there around dawn, maybe just past.

Hera plodded along dutifully. I like to believe that she's smarter than I think. Maybe she understood the importance of getting me home. Maybe she knew I was badly hurt. I don't know. At the very least, maybe she just wanted to go back to a barn where she knew she could be safe and commit fully to resting. Maybe she's just a horse, and she was doing what horses do—who knows? I like to believe she and I have a deeper connection, though. We probably don't, but don't take this dream from me. It felt like something greater than Fate to wake up and have her standing over me.

Letting her take the driving duties, I slipped my backpack off my shoulders and rooted through it for the tetracycline bottle. I swallowed more pills and another bottle of water. I drank two more bottles of water. The water was warm, but I didn't care. It moistened my dry mouth, and I was clearly in need of it. I also tugged down my waistband and changed out the dry, crusty bandage on my hip for a fresh one. I was encouraged that the wound did not start bleeding immediately, but I knew that it was a long way from healing.

Slow and steady, Hera walked toward home with a machine-like efficiency. Every step was a step closer to home. At least an hour passed. At that speed, I figured we covered three or four miles. She spooked a small pack of coyotes. The little dog-like scamps scattered, knowing full well that they would not do well against a healthy horse, or even an unhealthy horse. Coyotes were scavengers for a reason. I was no stranger to coyotes. They're all over the wilds of Wisconsin. I would see them on very rare occasions, usually as roadkill, but any time I was at a friend's bonfire at a house just outside of town, it wasn't uncommon to hear the yips and angst-ridden howls of the 'yotes. In Texas, the coyotes were everywhere. I saw them in the daytime and heard them in the nighttime on a near daily basis. They were much braver and bolder than the ones in Wisconsin.

In the distance, I could hear coyotes howling. Somewhere nearby, I heard a pack of dogs throw back their own howls, a cacophonous challenge, I suppose. The dog pack got Hera's attention. She twisted her head toward the direction of the howling and her ears went into full alert. I could feel her body tense beneath my legs. I patted her neck, trying to reassure her. "Easy, girl."

Another group of dogs threw up their own howls, even closer than the other group, and even louder. Hera wrenched her head to the left, and I felt her start to prance nervously. A large pack of dogs could take down a horse. The horse would let them know they were in a fight, but when they attacked the delicate legs of horse, they could eventually cripple the animal. Once the horse could not run or fight, it was done for. I had my shotgun. I wasn't about to let dogs take down my horse. I wondered how my firing the shotgun from her back would affect Hera, though. I had not had time to accustom her to gunfire. I know in the old cowboy movies, the heroes were always shooting their Winchesters from the saddle, but those horses had to be trained not to shy away from the sudden blast of a rifle. If it came to me having to shoot at a pack, I could easily see being dumped in a heap when Hera reared up and jumped to a run. I guess I would just have to deal with that if it came to it.

Beneath me, I could feel Hera getting more anxious and skittish. She started to bounce a little more, moving into a quicker walk that bordered on a slow trot. I felt twinges of pain shoot through my hip, but the rising adrenaline I was getting from the impending trouble negated it. I wrapped my left hand in a knot of mane and held the shotgun where the stock met the receiver with my right. Hera tensed suddenly. I could feel her starting to build for a run. I knew the dogs were closer than I thought.

When the pack rounded the corner, they were being led by a true monster, a beefy, thick, broad-headed Presa Canario. The dog looked well-fed and heavily muscled. Even in the dim light of the night sky, I could make our scars on its body and face gained from fighting, hunting, and squabbles to establish dominance. His ears were bobbed, so he had once been owned by someone. They stood up sharply on the sides of his head in a way that reminded me of Batman's cowl. The beast was followed by a cadre of smaller, but equally intimidating dogs. A couple of Staffordshire Bull Terriers, a German Shepherd, and a few motley stragglers of questionable breeding. The dogs were not in "hunt" mode. They seemed to be lollygagging and playing as they came around the corner of a nearby house. For a second, the dogs looked like happy-go-lucky pack that you'd find at a doggy daycare center.

The pack was not that large, and aside from the Shepherd, was not built for a speed. That made me feel moderately better. If we needed to outrun them, it seemed like a real possibility. They also did not seem to care that a man and a horse were standing within attack range of them. The big Presa in the lead spotted us right off. I saw him swivel his head at the horse, and his ears twitched. There was no heightening of excitement from the dog. He just continued his trot in our general direction. He did not tense or look like he was going to attack.

At this point, I had two choices: stand or run. Something, call it survival instinct, told me not to escalate the attack. I wasn't getting the sense that I was in danger. There wasn't a sense of hunger or challenge from the pack. They seemed to just be out being dogs, doing whatever it is a pack of feral dogs does when they're not starving. I knew that running would give them the excitement of motion. Dogs were action hunters. That's why they bolted without thinking when they saw a squirrel or a rabbit out of the corner of their eye.

Against the horse's wishes, I sank my hips back and pulled back on her mane. She tossed her head, but stopped walked. I could feel the muscles in her back tensing, readying to run if need be. She was a coiled spring. "Easy, girl." I patted her neck. "Trust me."

The pack was unhurried. It sauntered past us, the majority moving behind the horse, going on to wherever they were heading in their freedom. The Presa deviated from the pack, trotting toward the horse. Hera started to side-step nervously. I tried to soothe her, but Presa Canarios are *huge* dogs. He was easily more than half as tall as the horse, and probably went at least two-fifty or three hundred pounds. The Presa sniffed at Hera's rear leg, then sniffed at my boot. His head was massive. It was high enough that I could have given it pat if I wanted. The dog gave my foot a half-hearted lick with a sloppy, flat tongue, decided it didn't taste good, and returned to leading his pack. He didn't give me a second glance. They disappeared around the edge of another house.

I realized that I had been holding my breath. I exhaled, trembling from the exertion of not panicking. The horse was still on alert, her ears following the sound of the dogs. I nudged her with my heels, and she started forward. Her ears continued to twitch from side-to-side for a good mile until she determined that were a safe distance from the pack and let herself relax.

I slumped forward, leaning against her strong neck and giving her a vigorous rub. "Good horse. Good girl." She tossed her head as if she knew what I was saying, holding herself in a regal manner. I slapped her neck a few more times. "Let's go home."

With the sun starting to find the edge of the eastern sky, I started to recognize landmarks. We were not too far from the farm. *I'm coming, Ren.*

CHAPTER SEVENTEEN

You Will Be Fine

In my wildest dreams, the idea of being pregnant with twins had not occurred to me. Twins did not run in my family. I have no idea if they ran in Twist's family, or not. I just…well, I don't know what I thought. I guess I figured that if I was having twins I would have been twice as big as I was, and I was the size of a hot air balloon to begin with. I guess twins explained why they decided to come early. They ran out of space.

The labor for the little girl had taken so much out of me, though. It was like running a marathon, crossing the finish line, and then being told that you were going to have to run an additional half-marathon, too. I didn't know if I had it in me. I was exhausted to the point of crying. I wanted to sleep. I hurt all over. I was gripped by a blood-curdling sense of fear. I did not think I could do it. Horrible images of failing to birth this child swam through my mind. In the worst of the worst-case scenarios, Twist came home to find all three of us dead, me clutching the little girl to my chest, the other baby still stuck, unborn.

The sheer, grotesque horror of that visual picture seemed

to stimulate my adrenaline and refill some of my energy tanks. I told myself that it had to be easier the second time, right? The first baby had done the hard work of clearing the path. The other one just had to follow. I braced my feet against the wall at the foot of the tub like makeshift stirrups. I slid my butt down a little farther to get a better birthing angle, and tried not to crush the baby girl when I bore down to start pushing.

It did feel easier the second time. While I never felt the baby girl "moving" through the process, this time I could feel the second baby sliding a little easier. Don't get me wrong—it wasn't *that* much easier. The baby was still Twist's child, and had his giant-sized melon. I was still pushing a football-sized creature through a softball-sized opening. It was not *easy*, but it was easier than the first one.

I know, over the years, a lot was written about the strength of mothers before the Flu. My own mom had a refrigerator magnet that read, *You don't know true strength until you become a Mom.* I figured out what that meant right then and there. After my daughter slid out, I was exhausted beyond anything I had ever felt before. When I needed to get this second baby out, despite having no energy, and no measurable strength left, I somehow tapped a reserve I didn't know existed and found the ability to complete the birth. It took a few rounds of pushing, but I felt the head slide through. I had to balance my daughter on my chest while I reached down and pulled the second baby out of me, a baby boy! The prophesied Victor *was* in there! My Latina mother instinct was intact after all.

When I felt him slide free, my body was shivering from exhaustion. My muscles were seizing from dehydration and exertion. My stomach hurt. My pelvis hurt. I wanted to sleep more than anything I had ever wanted before, but the joy of having these babies out of me and in my presence kept me going.

I grabbed a fresh towel and brought the second baby

around to clean it, and then I froze. One of my worst case scenarios had come true. I saw the umbilical cord wrapped around his tiny neck. The baby was blue and swollen.

I screamed and started sobbing. I'd had even medical training to know when something was a lost cause, but I tried anyhow. I cut the cord free of its little neck, and I tried to breathe life into him, clearing his mouth and nose of mucus and fluids and trying to give him CPR. I slapped his back and tiny butt. I slapped the soles of his little feet. I pressed on his chest with my fingertips. I held his body to my ear and listened. I couldn't hear any heartbeat. I kept trying, anyhow.

I remember screaming curses to every god in the heavens. I remember crying. Babbling. Making impossible promises to whatever deity would come down and save my baby. None of them did. Scared, Fester ran out of the bathroom where he had been standing vigil on the sink. I scrambled out of the tub, laying the little girl on the floor next to my bed, where she immediately began wailing. She was alive. She could cry. She would be fine. My son, though—the son I had named after my poor, late father—he needed all the help I could give him.

I kept trying to prod and breathe life into little Victor. I desperately tried every measure available to me, but eventually, I had to stop. I could not do anything more. I had tried and failed. I lost. One of those horrible things that can happen had happened, I had been powerless to stop it, and I was going to have to play the hand that was dealt to me. I had no other choice. It was over. He was dead.

I wrapped Victor's little, still body in a towel like his sister. I could not stop sobbing. Every breath in my body was like prickling fire. The cold, logical part of my brain tried to convince me that it seemed ridiculous: I had anticipated one baby, I'd had one baby. Anything beyond that had not even been considered. There had been no promises. There had been no guarantees. I was silly to cry over a baby I hadn't even known had been there...but, yet...I could not stop crying. My son was dead.

I slipped on the adult diapers I'd picked up for just this situation to serve as a bandage post-birth. I wrapped myself in my heaviest robe. I picked up the squalling little girl and cradled her in my right arm. I picked up the tiny, blue-tinged body of Victor, swaddled like his sister, and I carried him in my left arm. I walked through the house, which somehow felt far less like my house than it had an hour ago. It felt tainted, somehow. Impure. Tarnished. Cursed.

I was in a dull, dead-eyed haze, not feeling anything except sorrow and agony. My heart felt like it was broken. No, that's not right. Not broken--shattered. It lay inside me in a million crystal shards, each with torn, jagged edges that bled me further. I stumbled through the house and into the backyard. The fire in the pit in the middle of the yard burned low. It was enough, though. I slumped in my chair in front of the fire and stared at the two bundles in my arms.

The little girl, desperately hungry, could sense breast milk nearby and rooted her head toward it blindly. I did not feel like feeding her, but I opened the front of my robe and let her latch on. Her cries ended immediately. I felt horribly guilty at that moment. Traumatically guilty. I felt like I had let my son die, and because of my grief over that, I was somehow unable to fathom that I had a healthy, living child that needed me.

I could not stop my tears. I felt like a dark cloud was settled over me. I ignored my daughter while I stared at the tiny, still face of my son, and I told him over and over that I was sorry. I apologized. I cuddled him to me, desperate to be his mother, desperate for him to know that he was loved, even though I had not even known he was going to be there. I could not stop saying I was sorry.

An hour passed. And then another. My daughter finished her feeding by falling into a deep, exhausted sleep. Swaddled against me, she slept peacefully, making tiny, shallow breaths. My body wanted to sleep, but my mind would not let it. My mind knew that my time with the little boy in my arms was limited. My mind was not going to miss a single second, no matter what my body demanded.

The sun pulled itself from the horizon. A wide swath of brilliant yellow light poured over the farm, lighting everything with a glowing aura. It made me angry. My son was dead, and the sky was turning into a brilliant blue as if nothing was wrong. It felt wrong. I wanted the sky to darken into a steely gray and pour rain down in sympathy for my pain.

The fire died to nearly embers, but it still radiated some heat. I could not bring myself to rouse out of the chair to put another log on it, though. I felt if I moved, I would have to go back to living. At that moment, I was suspended from life, hovering in a limbo state where I could simply be with my poor son.

I apologized through my tears to my daughter. I told her I was sorry that her mommy was not being a good mommy at that moment. I promised that I would change, that I would be the best mommy I could be to her, but she needed to give me this time with her brother. It would not last long. I almost envied the fact that she would be able to grow up and have no memories of her brother. I wished that I could say the same thing. I knew that I would never, ever forget a single second of his short time in my life, and I knew that it would always hurt me.

I hated that the sun was rising, that birds started singing, and that the pigs in the barn grunted in anticipation of their breakfast. I hated that the farm did not care that little Victor was dead, that the world did not care. I hated everything at that moment. I felt like I was alone in my grief, and would forever be alone.

I heard someone call my name. I could not find the strength to even look around at who was saying it. Was I hallucinating? Was I asleep? Was I dreaming? Who would be calling my name, anyhow? I saw a shadow out of the corner of my eye, but I could not tear my eyes from Victor.

I felt a hand on my shoulder, as familiar to me as breathing. Twist stood next to my chair. He said something, but his voice was hollow and empty. I could not hear him. I was frozen.

I felt his fingers touch my chin. He lifted my face. I wanted to resist, but I hadn't the strength left to do so. He was there. In the flesh. Next to me. I saw tears welling in his eyes. His mouth moved, but I heard no sound. He was leaning heavily on a walking stick. I saw a bloody bandage on his hip. Behind him, I saw Hera standing patiently, without saddle, bridle, or cart.

I had a million questions, but no desire to ask any of them. Instead, I looked him in the eye and started sobbing uncontrollably, the combined fatigue and emotional stress the past three days combining to wreck me.

Twist, with tears wet on his own cheeks, fell to his knees in front of me and wrapped me in his long arms. We sat there, the four of us, suspended from reality for an eternity. I tried to apologize, but I could not find the breath.

Twist pressed his face to the side of my head and whispered in my ear. "You will be fine. We will get through this."

Hearing my own mantra from him only made me cry harder. At that moment, I could not imagine a world in which I would ever be fine again.

CHAPTER EIGHTEEN

Hope for the Future

Since the Flu began, I have dug several graves. I buried my parents. I buried my high school girlfriend. I buried my dog, a woman who crossed my path, her crazed stalker, some feral dogs, and I filled in the grave of the man I met in Indiana when he passed from cancer. Each of those graves affected me deeply and changed me fundamentally, but none did it as profoundly as the grave I had to dig for my son.

There was the obvious physical pain of trying to dig a grave while still suffering the aftereffects of dehydration, hyperthermia, the infection in my side, and the damage from the shotgun blast, of course. But, that was minor compared to how much the idea of having to bury an infant hurt. I bled badly from my hip while I worked, but I would not stop. I got thick, angry blisters on my palms. I hurt all over, but the pain felt like it was proper for the situation. I ignored it. Something like this should never be a pain-free task.

I was going to bury him on the top of the little hill where I married his mother, but Ren stopped me from doing that. "Bury him at the base of the hill. We have a happy memory on the top of that hill, and we should not change that. At the base of the hill, we can still see him from the house."

I dug his grave at the base of the hill. It was not a grave that took a lot of time or strength, but yet it was the hardest thing I had ever done.

Two years ago, I put any thought of being a father out of my head. It seemed like it was something that would never happen. A year ago, I accept a life with Ren without children—who wants to bring children into a world without society? Only a few months ago, I learned I was going to be a father and my entire world changed. And now, I was going to have to bury one of my children.

Seeing Ren in the yard, her back to me, I had felt like I had returned home after a great and tragic journey. It felt like I had been gone for weeks, not days, and she was the beacon I had been following.

When I called her name and she did not move, I knew something was very wrong. When I slid off Hera's back and saw the two bundles in her arms, I was stunned, at first. Overjoyed. But when I approached and saw the differences between the two little faces, I knew what had happened. I stared at the healthy little girl, and then shifted to the son we had anticipated for so many weeks. Poor little Victor. I would never be able to teach him to hunt, or swim, or ride a horse. His short time on the Earth had passed before it even had a chance to begin.

Ren blamed herself for his death. I blamed myself. If I had been there to help, I maybe he would have lived. Maybe I could have gotten him out before...or, maybe it would have done no good at all.

I took my daughter from Ren's arms and clutched her to my chest. Ren refused to let me take Victor. She tightened her arm around him and shrugged my hand from her shoulder. I let her keep him.

She did allow me to help her from the chair and lead her to the house. I walked her to our bedroom and made her lay down. Our little girl, still asleep, I put into the bedside bassinet we'd prepared for the arrival. Ren continued to hold Victor. She fought sleep. I could see the exhaustion in her bleary, red-rimmed eyes. I could feel the exhaustion in my own.

I turned to leave, and for the first time since I got home, I heard Ren say something other than *I'm sorry.* "Where are you going?"

I turned to face her. "I am going to dig a grave for Victor." Each word out of my throat felt like knives cutting soft tissues. They burned and bled as I said them. I choked on the blood in my throat.

Ren's face went through a whirlwind of potential reactions, twisting first from outrage, to sadness, to acceptance. She inhaled sharply and nodded. Nothing she could do could change what happened, so we could only press forward. "Yes." She nodded again and hugged the little boy closer to her chest. "Please do."

There was a pause between us. Tears burned hot at the corners of my eyes, but I tried not to let them fall. I wanted to be strong for Ren, and for our little girl, even though I was dying inside.

"Make sure you put him somewhere in the sun. I want him to be in the sun."

I held my son for the first, and last time, as we prepared him for burial. After I dug the grave, I assembled a hasty coffin out of pine boards I had in the garage. I made a simple box and hammered it together in short order. I used a chisel to carve his name on the lid. I lined the coffin with a cartoon baseball-player comforter we had intended for his bed. I put a tiny pillow at one side. Ren dressed him in a cute little blue-and-white outfit that she said reminded her of an old sweater her father used to wear. After the baby was dressed, she wrapped him in a blanket again and let me hold him for the first time. I sat in a chair at the table in the kitchen. No more tears came. The physical exertion of grieving while digging his grave had taken them from my body. "He's handsome."

"Like his father." Ren held our daughter, who was feeding again.

After the little girl had eaten, Ren dressed her in a little dress that was in one of the many bags of baby clothes she had scavenged from homes in the area. She wrapped her in a blanket to keep her warm, despite the Texas heat.

When Ren, herself, had dressed in a simple black dress, she cleared her throat and announced, "I'm ready now."

I carried Victor to the grave where his little coffin lay waiting. Ren carried our little girl. We said goodbye to the baby who never had a chance. We hugged him and kissed him one last time. I placed him on the little bed I had prepared in the coffin. Ren cried over him some more, but our grief was ebbing. We would never forget him. We would never stop grieving him. But, we would adjust. We would continue to survive. Victor's sister needed us now. We had to acknowledge that, and we had to keep pressing forward.

I nailed the cover onto the little coffin. Each tap of the hammer hurt. The sound of the nailing scared my daughter and she cried and fussed until it was done. I lowered the little coffin into the ground, and my heart broke again when it gently thumped onto the cold clay far below.

I used the shovel to help me stand again. My hip was throbbing. "Should we say something?" I wanted to provide him with a fitting eulogy, but no words were coming to me.

Ren wet her lips. "This baby…he is for my parents, and for your parents. They should have been here to share in the joy of a new birth. They should have been here to hold their granddaughter, but since they cannot, we send them their grandson. They will watch over him for us, until we can be there with him ourselves, wherever that might be."

The lump in my throat felt like it was going to choke me. I swiped at my eyes with the back of my forearm. I had to fight to produce words. "I'm sure my parents would like that."

"Your mom is going to have to physically fight my mom to hold him. Hell hath no fury like someone who stands between a Venezuelan *abuela* and her grandchild." The corners of Ren's mouth twisted into the briefest of smiles, but it fled all too quickly.

"My dad would have made him watch Notre Dame football games."

"My dad would have made him be a Mets fan. Screw the Yankees."

"I never got to see him alive, but I love him more than I thought I could love anything."

Ren looked down at the little girl in her arms. "We will have to love his sister twice as much now. We have to make up for what we cannot give him."

I looked down at the little pink face in the soft, angora blanket. "I don't think that will be a problem."

I stuck the shovel into the pile of dirt next to the grave. "Goodbye, Victor. I love you." I turned the spade of earth upside down and the hollow down of dirt on the coffin seemed to echo through my heart, and through the sky.

Ren crouched and grabbed a handful of dirt, casting it down into the grave. "I love you, too. I wish you could have stayed here with me."

Then, one shovelful after another, I filled in the grave. Ren and the baby watched until I was done. When the last spade of dirt was dropped, I smoothed over the scar in the ground at the base of the hill, and I dropped the shovel into the grass.

Ren fell toward me, and we hugged each other fiercely. We still felt real to each other, even though nothing else did at that very second. Our grief was a lead weight that threatened to crush us both, but we sought for strength in each other. We clutched at each other and shared our sadness. She was there for me, and I tried to be there for her, despite the choking fog of sorrow. It was just the two of us—now three with the baby in Ren's arms—against the world. Even if that was all we would ever have, at that moment it was more than enough.

I fed and pastured the animals. Ren told me of her battle with the lion. I told her of Enrique's clan, and of Chet, and how Hera found me and helped me get home. Ren told me about giving birth. When the baby was fed and sleeping, we napped as best we could. Neither of us *wanted* sleep, but the physical and mental tolls had worn our bodies to a breaking point. We caught light naps here and there, both of us waking to check on the baby frequently. No chores were done that day, outside of the necessary care of the animals. No real meals were made. We snacked, instead. All food tasted bland. I made Ren drink plenty of water. She made me drink plenty of water. We started the long process of healing, both physically and emotionally.

"I wish we could have had a picture of him."

"I will never forget what he looked like." Ren adjusted the blanket over the baby's legs. "He looked like you."

I stood over the little bassinet next to our bed and drank in every detail of my daughter. Every little crease in her peaceful face, every curve in her arms and legs, the little chin that echoed her mother's chin, and the stubby little nose that looked far too much like my father's nose. The baby sighed in her sleep. Her little arms, wavered for a second, reaching out in front of her. I reached down and touched the little fingers, covered by a thin piece of fabric built into the little infant pajamas. "Daddy is here."

From the bed, propped up on pillow, Ren said, "We can't call her 'the baby' forever. She will eventually need a name."

"I guess I was sold on having a son," I said.

"You do. You will always have a son, even if he can't be

with us."

"I know. I guess I just never even bothered to consider a different name, let alone a girl's name."

"We're going to have to come up with one. We could name her after your mother, or my mother, or my sister?"

I shrugged. "Maybe."

"Do you have a better suggestion? I never thought about it, either."

I rest my hand lightly over the baby's chest and stomach. I felt the barely-noticeable rise-and-fall of her breathing. She was strong. Healthy. It made me feel better about the future. I looked at Ren, who had never been more beautiful than she was at that very moment. "We could name her after the one thing we will always have."

"What's that?"

"Hope."

It's Thursday, I think. Honestly, it doesn't matter.

The days themselves are unimportant. I count time by the growth of a little girl now. She's forty-eight days old as I write this, strong, healthy, and growing like a weed. I have been making check marks to count the days in my journals. I want to remember her birthday. I want to remember everything about her.

Little Hope is everything I wanted her to be, and then some. The more she grows, the more excited I am to see what the next day will bring. Granted, she is not much right now outside of being a sleeping, eating, and pooping machine, but I am embracing that fully, enjoying her for what she is and gratefully anticipating what she will become.

Ren and I struggle some days, but the joy that Hope has brought into our lives helps. We cannot change what we cannot change. That has become our motto. Someday, if I ever make a placard for this farm, that will be the motto on a ribbon below the coat of arms.

I think of the little boy at the bottom of the hill often, and I hope that he is with my parents, and with Ren's parents, and I hope he is happy there. Perhaps someday I will get to meet him again. Maybe I won't.

In the meantime, I survive. So does Ren. So does Hope. We have a farm to run. We have food to grow, water to purify, and solar panels to assemble, erect, and wire so that our house can have electricity again. There are a million things that I need to do, and we have a future to build.

This is the continued journal of my life.

My name is Twist. I'm twenty. I'm a husband, a father, and farmer. I have a beautiful wife, Renata, and a daughter, Hope.

And we are still alive.

Acknowledgements

Three books. Who knew I could do it?

This book goes out to everyone who liked the first two. Without your support, I never would have made it this far. Thank you to those of you who read the first two in this series, thanks to those of you who bought copies or came to signings, and thanks to those of you who liked the first two enough to ask for a third. This is truly your book. Please, tell friends, write reviews, and tell your libraries to get copies. It helps more than you know.

I'd like to take a second to thank the people who have helped me, who have said nice things about my work, and the people who have believed.

Paige Krogwold did the cover for this book, just as she did the other two in this series, and it was fantastic, as usual.

Ann Hayes, Veronika Linins, Maddy Hunter, and Jack Quincey were my beta-readers. Their feedback was invaluable.

Thanks to everyone at Mystery to Me. Their support has meant a lot to me. I always enjoy stopping in there. That store makes me wish I lived closer to downtown so I could stop in more often.

Thanks to my sister, Erin, and my buddies, Dusty and Ryan. We played a lot of *Call of Duty* at night, and that's why it took me longer to write this book. I greatly appreciated the distraction, and look forward to more distraction.

Thanks to my wife, Kaija, for her support and friendship, and to daughter, Annika, for my giving me the impetus to write about birth. *(Now, stop watching YouTube and go read a book.)*

Thanks to my parents. They don't always understand my sense of humor, but they are to blame for my love of reading and writing. My mom bought me the "Dragonlance Chronicles" for Christmas when I was six. Those three books pretty much doomed me to a life of nerdly pursuits and writing.

I guess I could thank Margaret Weis for writing the "Dragonlance" books, too.

And finally, a heavy shout-out and double-stacked load of gratitude with cheese to the fine people at wonderful Culver's restaurant in Sun Prairie where 100 percent of this book was written, and about 80 percent of it was edited. Stop in and tell them I sent you. You won't get a discount or anything. They might even look at you strangely, like perhaps you need therapy. But, nonetheless, go buy a burger from them and tell them thanks. If enough people do this, maybe we can get Culver's to sponsor the next book.

--Hey, a guy can dream.

Sun Prairie, Wis.
June 2018

About the Author

Sean Patrick Little lives in Sun Prairie, Wisconsin. He writes a lot. He watches too much TV. He plays guitar and bass badly. He has two cats that annoy him a lot. He has a dog, a walleyed, big-eared Heeler/Corgi mix, who demands constant belly rubs. He has a wife and a child.

That child has recently become a teenager.

Please send help.

You can follow Sean on Goodreads, Twitter, Tumblr, and Facebook if you are interested in keeping up with his upcoming projects. He is not hard to find.

He's not terribly exciting, but he enjoys the attention all the same. Since he had to give up eating starches and sugar, tiny rations of attention is all that keeps him going anymore.

Facebook: facebook.com/seanpatricklittlewriter
Twitter: @WiscoWriterGuy

Other Books by Sean Patrick Little

The Centurion: The Balance of the Soul War
The Seven
*Longrider: Away From Home**
*Longrider: To the North**
*The Bride Price**
*Without Reason**

The Survivor Journals

After Everyone Died
Long Empty Roads
All We Have
*--The Survivor Journals Omnibus**

The TeslaCon Novels

Lord Bobbins and the Romanian Ruckus
Lord Bobbins and the Dome of Light (coming 2018)
Lord Bobbins and the Clockwork Girl (coming 2018)

All books are available as eBooks on your favorite online retailers. Hard copies can be ordered online or, preferably, through your favorite independent bookstore. Remember: local stores need your support more than major online retailers do.

*E-book only

Publisher's Note

The world of publishing grows more and more competitive every year. It is harder and harder for small press and independent books to compete in a crowded marketplace. There is a mountain of books published annually and only so many readers and so many hours in a day for people to read — not to mention the almost insurmountable competition from all the various electronic screens that beg people's interest and attention.

If you enjoyed this book, please help us spread the word about it. Tell all your friends. If they buy copies and like it, ask them to tell their friends, and their friends' friends, and so on. Word of mouth is always the best sales tool.

If you are a creative type, doing things like posting fan art on social media, participating in message boards and plugging the book, doing cosplay and posting photos, or making models of things in the book is greatly appreciated. Use hashtags to make sure people know where the inspiration for the image originated and to what it relates. Anything that extends the reach and audience of the book is always a positive and always appreciated. Support the things you enjoy.

To further aid the cause, you can politely ask your local library to purchase a copy and ask your local bookstores to carry it, as well. Every little bit helps.

If you enjoyed this book, please leave a kind review on major websites like Amazon or Goodreads, or any of your other favorite book retailers. Link to the book on your Facebook pages or Twitter accounts. Good, honest reviews help more than you know, and we truly appreciate every review. The more positive reviews the book gets, the farther the reach of the book spreads.

If you have a bookstore or work in a library and want one of our authors to speak, or you would like to host a signing, please let us know. If we can make it happen, we will.

And if you really enjoyed this book, please let the author know. A kind word is sometimes the jolt a writer needs to keep working. That goes for any book you've enjoyed, ever. Most writers are on Twitter nowadays. Or they have email addresses or some other way to contact them. If you send them a message, they will see it. They might not reply, but they will be grateful.

You should probably also do the same things for anyone important in your life in general: your grandmother or grandfather, your parents, a favorite teacher, a friend that has been there for you—it really doesn't matter: If someone has done something that you have appreciated, please let them know.

Spread some positivity in this world. It will do you, and others, more good than you might know.

With sincere gratitude,
Spilled Inc. Press

CPSIA information can be obtained
at www.ICGtesting.com
Printed in the USA
FSHW022006220620
71458FS